Border City Chronicles

Edmond Gagnon

Copyright © 2019 Edmond Gagnon

ISBN: 9781-99928-14-1-0

All rights reserved. No part of this publication may be reproduced, stored in a retrieval system, or transmitted in any form or by any means, electronic, mechanical, recording or otherwise, without the prior written permission of the author.

Printed on acid-free paper.

Although this book was inspired by real events, the characters and stories told are fictitious. Any similarity to real persons, living or dead, is strictly coincidental and not intended by the author. Any opinions expressed in this book are solely his and do not represent the opinions of the publisher on others.

2019

First Edition

Border City Chronicles

Other Books by Edmond Gagnon

A Casual Traveler

Rat

Bloody Friday

Torch

Finding Hope

All These Crooked Streets

Four

www.edmondgagnon.com

Edmond Gagnon

Dedication

This book is for a man who passed before his time. A man who was proud of his son, but like most men had difficulty telling him so. Instead, he leant a hand or shared old stories and laughs while fishing or over beer and wings. He was cherished by his family and friends and everyone who knew him. One of the stories in this book took place in his old stomping grounds—where he lived, worked, and socialized. Everybody affectionately called him Wiener.

This one's for you, dad. I miss you!

Edmond Gagnon

Acknowledgements

For every book that is written there is a group of people behind the scenes that help. Anyone who puts their mind to it can write a book. Creating one that's well-written and looks professional is a different story. If an author wants the book read the story has to be interesting with a plot that works and characters that are believable.

By the time I send a manuscript to the printer I've read it a dozen times or more. There are adjustments and re-writes and edits to be considered. Once satisfied its worthy, I send it off to beta readers for input and opinion. After fine tuning it I send it to my editor. When it comes back from her, I check the editing.

Then the manuscript had to be formatted into a book template with an index and/or numbered pages. My publisher checks the formatting while I work with a cover designer. I incorporate my own photos for a sense of recognition and realism.

The publisher wraps the cover around the formatted book, sends it to the printer, and ships me a proof copy. Then I have to read the entire book again to check for errors or omissions and overall quality. By that time, I'm sick of reading it and ready for a beer.

I'd personally like to thank Rebecca Gagnon, Darcel Goetz, Donna Morykot, Domonique Jean, and Emily Conran Andrews for their help. As always, I have to thank my wife Cathryn for coming to my rescue when I'm ready to throw the computer out the window.

This book was edited by Christine Hayton. It's amazing how many things she found wrong after I thought I had a finished manuscript.

Edmond Gagnon

'Baby Shay' 10

'Designated Hitters' 83

'Knock-Out' 123

Border City Chronicles

'Baby Shay'

One

She's Gone!

Jolene shouted at Kenny. "Turn that down, its Shay's nap time and I gotta pick up my mom."

The UFC announcer couldn't describe the human carnage quick enough as Dan Severn pounded the other fighter into submission. His opponent's face was unrecognizable, cut and bloodied from the rapid succession of vicious blows.

Kenny gulped his beer and yelled. "Kill him!" He paid no mind to Jolene, punched the air with his fist, and mimicked his hero on the tube.

Jolene snatched the remote on her way to the bedroom and lowered the volume. Taking quick stock of the empty bottles on the coffee table, she saw her man was seven beers into the two-four he'd brought home for the weekend. He ignored her whenever he watched sports or played video games. She knew better than to disturb him.

Jolene entered the bedroom and placed Shay in her crib. The baby had just finished a bottle and was nodding off. She smoothed her daughter's silky red hair with her fingertips. The rusty color was a sore point with Kenny, and he questioned whether he was Shay's real father.

Although born premature six months earlier, the baby was only slightly shy of her proper weight. Jolene gave her daughter a pacifier and tucked a blanket around her.

With the baby down for the afternoon, she turned to tidy herself in the mirror. Her brown hair had gotten long, reaching half way down her back. It was oily and in need of a wash, but she didn't have enough time. She wanted to cut it but feared the grief she'd get from Kenny. He liked it long and told her to grow it to her ass. He thought that style was sexy.

The TV's volume increased. Kenny had turned it up. Jolene closed the bedroom door. She pulled off her soiled shirt and plucked her favourite tank top from a hook in the closet. Unable to fluff her oily hair, she tucked it behind her ears.

Her reflection in the mirror prompted a frown. She'd always hated how her top ribs protruded further than her small and shapeless breasts. She'd thought the pregnancy might help, but it didn't. Kenny always needled her about it.

Turning for the door, Jolene tripped over his discarded clothes. The small room was cluttered with their furniture and the baby's crib. She scooped up his stuff and tossed everything into the closet. It seconded as a clothes hamper.

Adjusting the curtains to keep the direct sunlight away from Shay, she closed the door on her way out of the bedroom. As she manoeuvred around the coffee table, Kenny held up an empty beer bottle. This was his cue for her to fetch him another, but his gaze never strayed from the squawk box.

"Will you keep an ear open for Shay?"

Jolene grabbed the beer and handed him another Labatt's Blue.

"I'm going to pick up mom, do you want me to bring you a burger for dinner?"

He took a hit off the open bottle and waved her off.

Jolene stepped off her porch and filled her lungs with the closest thing to fresh air Windsor's west end could offer. That section of the city stood downwind from the steel mill on Detroit's Zug Island. It was mid-June and summer had arrived.

Picking up her mom, meant a trip to the Chippewa Tavern. The neighborhood watering hole about halfway between her house on Bloomfield, and her mother's place on Baby Street. Other than at home, the Chip was the only place her mother drank. Welfare cheques were in so she would be there for sure.

The bar did a brisk business with patrons cashing their government checks. It quickly filled with the usual suspects. The regulars had their own seats. Mom's was at the far end of the bar, near the bathroom. The distance was convenient given her weak bladder. Jolene sat beside her on the only empty stool at the bar, no one dared take that reserved seat. Everyone feared the wrath of Joyce Lockwood.

Jolene never cared for the Chip. Her father was stabbed and killed there in a senseless fight. She didn't drink much, but sometimes nursed a glass of white wine while she waited for her mother. Joyce usually hit the bar around noon, in time for a liquid lunch. The draft beer and shot of whiskey in front of her were her two best friends.

She slurred. "Hey honey...I shaved a sheet for ya."

The country music from the Juke box was stifled by the cacophony of loud chatter in the room. Jolene couldn't make out the song, but the melody sounded familiar. Kenny liked hard rock, but honky-tonk was more her style. She loved Tim McGraw, thought he was cute.

The Chippewa Tavern was over a hundred years old; a blind pig during prohibition, and a reputed hangout for Chicago gangster Al Capone. The neon signs and memorabilia from beer companies that hung on the nicotine-stained walls were barely visible through the cloud of cigarette smoke.

Jolene was embarrassed by her drunken mother. The bartender automatically placed a glass of white wine in front of her. Failure to do so would have gotten him a tongue-lashing from Juice, her mother's nickname at the bar. Being a regular, whose husband had been killed there, she acted like a celebrity who owned the place.

Jolene placed an order with the kitchen so she wouldn't have to make dinner at home. She lacked the groceries and knowhow, having learned nothing from her mother. Joyce usually covered her daughter's tab, a big spender with taxpayer's money.

Waiting patiently, Jolene listened to her mother incoherently try to solve what ailed the world. It was time to leave, before her legs gave out and Jolene would have to stuff her into a taxi cab. After three stumbles and one near fall on the walk to her mother's house, Jolene plopped her onto the sofa. She turned the on the TV and placed a beer beside the remote.

Arriving back home, Jolene heard the head-banging music before she got to her door. Kenny was exactly where she'd left him, on the couch with his head fallen back and mouth wide open. He was down for the count. She eyed the collection of empties, now doubled, and turned off the music. The bedroom door was closed, and Shay was quiet.

Silence was rare with the baby being colicky and crying all the time. Kenny always bitched about the noise and Jolene barely slept.

She took a deep breath and opened the bedroom door, but there wasn't a sound. She peeked into the crib. Shay wasn't there. Time stood still, until it registered with her. Jolene turned back toward the living room and screamed, "Kenny, she's gone!"

Two

Where's My Baby?

Hysterical, Jolene screamed, "Where's my baby...where's Shay?"

Kenny slowly came to, as if he'd been in a year-long coma. In his drunken stupor, he tried to focus on the two women who stood in front of him; both Jolene.

"Where is she...you're supposed to be watching her."

He rubbed his glazed eyes and stared at the woman on the right until the other one disappeared.

"Wha-whadaya talkin about? I just checked her."

"She's not here, see for yourself."

He pulled himself up from the couch, keeping one hand on it for balance. Kenny staggered into the bedroom and peered into the crib.

"She's not here."

"No shit...where's Shay, Kenny?"

Acting as if the infant had somehow climbed out of her own crib, he searched underneath it and their bed.

"You idiot, she can barely crawl, let alone get out of her crib. When did you last check on her?"

"I dunno. I guess I fell asleep."

He stumbled around the room, looking under clothes on the floor.

"She couldn't have gotten far."

"What's the matter with you? She didn't go anywhere on her own. Someone took her while you were zonked out."

He didn't comprehend the gravity of the situation.

"Maybe your mom picked her up."

"I was with my mom, you moron."

"I meant my mom...maybe she..."

Jolene cut him off.

"When's the last time your mom saw Shay? She hates her own kids, you know that."

Kenny parted the curtains with one hand and gazed out the bedroom window.

"Maybe she got outside, somehow."

Jolene shook her head in disgust and stormed into the living room. "Someone took my baby...I'm calling the cops."

She couldn't remember the conversation. She stood and stared out the front door, shaking. Kayla, the woman who resided in the other half of their duplex, stuck her face in the screen door.

"What's goin' on girl, did I hear you say someone took the baby?"

"Kenny was supposed to be watching her, but he passed out. Did you hear anything?"

"Just her crying, but nothing unusual. How did he sleep through that?"

"You'd be surprised, he does it every night."

Kayla let herself in the door.

"You're shaking like a leaf; can I get you something...a shot of whiskey or a pill? Darrell's got downers in the cupboard."

"No, the cops are on their way."

"Who the hell would take your baby? That's sick. I'll be right back. I gotta open some windows to get rid of the weed smell before Five-O gets here."

Jolene remained standing in the doorway, waiting for the police. Tears flowed freely down her face; her arms too weak to wipe them away. She glanced over her shoulder at Kenny on the couch doing head-bobs, trying to stay awake.

"Maybe you should throw cold water on your face, before the cops see how drunk you are."

"I was tired, it's not my fault I fell asleep. Maybe YOU should get a job and try working all week. I was just enjoying my day off."

"Maybe YOU should pay a little more attention to our daughter. I'm the one who..."

A police cruiser pulled to the curb out front. Another one came up the street from the other direction. A female cop got out of the first car. A police Sergeant parked his vehicle facing the first car, and the two officers walked up the sidewalk to the porch.

Jolene froze in the doorway. The Sergeant asked questions while the Constable took notes. "You called about a missing baby?"

Still shaking and her face soaked with tears, she stuttered her words.

"Sh-Shay, m-my baby girl...someone t-took her f-from her bed...in the house."

"Do you mind if we come in and have a look around?"

"We've already looked. Sh-she's only s-six months and can't c-climb out of the c-crib on her own."

"I understand, but we still have to look around."

Kenny appeared from the bathroom. His brown hair was wet and freshly combed back, but his eyes said he was either stoned or on an all-night bender. His skinny, tattooed arms poked out of his black tee shirt like colored toothpicks. The thin moustache he'd been trying to grow all his life resembled a sickly caterpillar.

Jolene spoke up.

"This is my boyfriend, Kenny. Shay is our daughter. He was watching her while I was out, but he fell asleep, and someone took her from her crib in the bedroom."

The Sergeant eyeballed Kenny like he was on the ten most wanted list. "Sir, please give this officer your full name and birth date, while your girlfriend shows me where the baby was last seen."

"What do you need that for? Shouldn't you be out looking for our baby?"

The supervisor didn't respond, he nodded Jolene towards the bedroom. The Constable took a step closer to Kenny.

"Sir, we need the information, so we know what to look for, and where. I'll also need the names of all your family members, and any neighbours that you know?"

In the bedroom, Jolene pointed out the empty crib. The Sergeant swivelled his head to take in the tiny, cluttered room. He leaned forward to peer into the closet.

"Kenny already looked in there, but I told him Shay's not capable of getting out of her crib."

"So where were you when she went missing?"

"At the Chippewa. I went there to get my mother and take her home. I put Shay to sleep before I left. Kenny was watching TV. He said he'd keep an eye on her, but he was sleeping on the couch when I got home."

The Sergeant parted the curtains and gazed out the window. "And what time was that?"

"I don't know...maybe five minutes before I called you. She was gone and I freaked out. The neighbour said she heard Shay crying but didn't see anything unusual."

"Okay, give her name to the other officer. We'll be canvassing the neighbourhood. Is it possible a family member took the baby without telling you?"

Jolene clenched her hands and pressed them into her stomach. All the color had drained from her face.

"No... I don't know anyone who would...I think I'm gonna be sick." She bolted passed the Sergeant, for the bathroom.

He walked into the living room where the Constable was taking notes. Kenny, dazed, slouched on the couch. The veteran cop studied the skinny kid, not impressed with his demeanour.

"Are there any rooms we haven't seen yet?"

Kenny stared at a picture of Shay on the coffee table. A circle of beer bottles surrounded the photo like sentinels.

"This is it. I looked everywhere already."

"It looks like someone's had a few beers."

"Yeah, so what. It's my day off and I'm in my own house. What's wrong with that?"

"Nothing. Unless someone took your child while you got drunk and fell asleep."

Kenny broke from his trance and glared at the Sergeant.

"I didn't do anything wrong. Like I said, maybe you should be out looking for my baby."

"That's what we're going to do, young man. We'll broadcast the child's description, search the neighbourhood, and talk to everyone you know. Do you have a picture of your baby we could have?"

"Take that one." Kenny lifted his chin to the Sergeant, signalling him to take the framed photograph on the table.

Three

Dukes of Hazard

"I've got the eye. Can you guys plug in at opposite ends of the block, in case he makes a run for it?"

Norm Strom had started his afternoon shift early, and left instructions with his boss to brief the other drug squad members, before they joined him on the stakeout.

He'd received a tip from a confidential informant that a quarter pound of cocaine would be delivered to a well-known drug dealer on Queen Street, in the west end. The information was good. The source had proven himself on two previous occasions, netting the cops weed, coke, cash and a handgun.

The dealer who lived in the targeted house was waiting on a new supply. There were no grounds to obtain a search warrant. Norm's CI bought dope from him. The informant supplied a description of the deliveryman and his vehicle but didn't have a name.

The police radio squawked with two separate transmissions:

"Hawk's set up on the nine side." and "Maverick's got the three."

It was code for west and east. Storm (Norm's handle) backed his Toyota Camry into the driveway of an abandoned hair salon across and two houses down the street. He was *the eye,* he had the target in sight, and was in position to report any movement.

Doing surveillance in plain clothes was a lot different than driving around in a marked police car. Officers were able to blend in by growing their hair long and dressing down to fit the occasion. Hawk looked like a washed-out football player who normally donned sports attire. Maverick had the appearance of a Colombian cartel member, with a foo-Manchu and hair half-way down his back.

Norm Strom didn't look as grungy as some of his fellow Drug Squad officers, but his casual dress and demeanor helped him go unnoticed when he needed to. That was the idea, not to stand out or look like a cop.

His stomach growled. Lunch had been hours earlier, and dinner would have to wait until after the arrest, if one was made. The Drug Squad called it a street mugging; a term used when they took down a suspect in public.

The legal grounds to make such an arrest were far less than those needed to search a private residence. If the suspect was committing a criminal offence a warrant wasn't needed to affect an arrest.

After an uneventful hour of seeing nothing but a few kids chasing a dog, a marked police cruiser drove by. Norm changed the radio channel to the patrol frequency in case someone had reported his car as suspicious. It wouldn't have been the first time that had happened.

He heard chatter on the radio and listened as the west side Sergeant broadcasted information about a missing baby. *That's great,* he thought, *more cop cars to scare off the delivery guy.* Norm radioed the other two cars on his drug frequency and gave them a heads up on the baby situation.

Maverick responded. "Copy that, Storm, should we break off and help with the search?"

The drug cop had a young child at home and undoubtedly felt the parents' pain.

"Not yet. Let's give this another half hour. In the mean time I'll call in and get more details about what's going on."

Minutes later, while Norm was on the phone with the dispatcher, the suspect vehicle pulled into the driveway at the dealer's house. The communication centre was already aware of the Drug Squad's location. He gave them the make and model of the vehicle they were about to stop.

Norm radioed the others.

"Target arrived; I'll block him in."

He threw the handheld radio onto the passenger seat. The suspect had one foot out of his car when Norm pulled in behind him. A quick glance over his shoulder and he fell back into his black Chrysler. He reversed and rammed the front end of Norm's Toyota, buckling its hood.

The suspect's vehicle pushed Norm's backwards, and into the street. When the two cars came to a stop, Norm reached for the door handle. Maverick was nearby on foot. He sprinted across the front lawn toward the Chrysler. Unable to exit the driveway, the suspect drove forward toward Maverick. The cop lunged at the driver through the open car window and grabbed him by the arm.

Norm got out of his car and saw Maverick had the suspect in a headlock. The Chrysler moved forward, across the lawn. Hawk drove up and tried to cut off the fleeing vehicle at the street, but the suspect manoeuvred around him and the other cars that were parked along the curb. The driver continued his escape, dragging Maverick along with him.

Hawk reversed his car down the street in another attempt to cut off the suspect. He overshot his mark and the Chrysler made it onto the roadway. With his car out of commission, Norm ran towards the suspect vehicle. Maverick still had a hold of the driver as the car fled in the opposite direction. Hawk stopped to turn around, and Norm jumped in with him.

Norm radioed the dispatcher for uniformed assistance. Police pursuits in unmarked vehicles was strictly forbidden, but there was no way he could call off the chase while his comrade was being dragged by a lunatic in a speeding automobile.

At the east end of the block, the suspect turned left, and then right into an alley. Maverick almost slipped under the car in the first turn, the next one sent his legs flying into the air. The driver veered toward a telephone pole, to ditch the cop.

He barely avoided the pole, then fishtailed to the right. His tires slipped and spun in the grass-covered alley. Maverick broke free, hit the ground, and rolled into a hedgerow. Hawk and Norm slowed to check on him, but Maverick waved them on. It appeared he was okay.

The suspect car never let up. A puff of white powder flew from the driver's window, as he tried to ditch the evidence. When the driver got to the end of the alley, a police cruiser blocked his path. He veered left and drove through a chain link fence. With nowhere else to go, the Chrysler smashed into the back porch of a private residence.

The driver bailed and fled on foot. Like sharks on fresh bait, uniformed cops swarmed and tackled him. He was handcuffed, and pinned face-first on the ground, when Norm arrived. The Narc chuckled when they rolled the man over. Cocaine powder covered his face and chest. Norm suggested the officers avoid inhaling.

Hearing a familiar voice behind him, Storm turned around and saw Maverick charging forward.

"Where is that fucker? I'm gonna kill him."

Maverick was bloodied, bruised, and limping. It was a good thing the uniforms had already taken the suspect away.

Hawk looked at his co-worker and shook his head.

"Rookie move, Mav, didn't anyone ever warn you about riding on the outside of a moving vehicle?"

"But I had him. I almost choked him out."

Storm chimed in.

"Yeah, and you almost wore that telephone pole in the alley. Go to the hospital with Hawk and get checked out. If they don't keep you for the night, you're buying beer and pizza. He didn't dump all the evidence, we found three ounces of coke in the car."

One of the uniformed officers called out to Norm.

"Dispatch is trying to get you on channel one."

Four

Day Two

It was Norm's forty-ninth lap on the riding lawn mower, he was about halfway through the near acre of grass, when his pager vibrated the roll of flesh that bulged from the top of his pants. He reached down to retrieve the mobile device, then drove to the back door and shut the mower down.

Using the cordless extension phone, he checked his voicemail. The message was from William Clark, one of the Staff Sergeants who oversaw the Criminal Investigations Branch (CIB).

Curious about the brief call, Norm wondered what Wild Bill could possibly want. The man was a legend in his own time. Relentless as a bloodhound, Clark was notorious for his work ethic and ability to solve homicides. His men idolized him. The police brass loved his results but cringed at the overtime hours he generated.

When questioned about the huge expenditure on one murder investigation, Clark told the Chief that he should be the one to tell the victim's family how the police couldn't afford to investigate their personal loss. Administration never questioned him about the extra hours again.

Norm had never worked directly for Wild Bill, but the man approached him once, regarding a suspect in custody for breach of parole. He was an informant of Clark's, who introduced him to Norm so he could trade drug information for a get out of jail free card.

Norm interviewed the informant and received information on five different drug dealers. He was able to make arrests and narcotics seizures in three of the cases. Wild Bill was happy that his CI came through with enough to facilitate his release. Norm scored Brownie points with the Staff Sergeant.

His call to Clark was picked up by the secretary and transferred to the legend. He answered in his usual gruff tone.

"Normie, come in and see me. I need your help."

Bill Clark was one of only a few people who ever called him Normie.

"I'm on afternoons, I can see you..."

"Come in now, I cleared it with your boss."

Wild Bill cut him off and hung up. Norm stood there with phone in hand, puzzled. He wiped sweat from his brow with the back of his forearm and looked at the uncut grass.

"Shit!"

When Norm walked into the CIB office Clark was at his desk, barking at someone else on the phone.

"No, like I told the last two bloodsuckers...no comment."

He slammed down the receiver and pointed to a television mounted on the wall.

"Did you see this shit? All the major U.S. news crews are here. Those kids called the media about their missing baby. Claim we aren't doing shit to find her."

The Criminal Investigations Branch was unusually quiet. The desk man, a senior detective, listened to someone on the phone while he watched the news. Norm stared at the television in disbelief. He couldn't recall ever seeing American media on the Canadian side of the border. He waited for Wild Bill to calm down. His face resembled an overripe tomato about to explode.

"What can I do to help?"

"You got people on the west end, Normie. Any good finks?"

He thought for a second.

"A couple, why?"

Clark stabbed his index finger at the TV and then the phone.

"This thing hasn't stopped ringing, and everyone wants to know what we're doing about the missing baby. The Chief will be in here any minute. He wasn't pleased at the morning meeting, when he heard about the child.

Work your sources and beat the bushes. Dig into the parents, the family, and even the pet dog if they've got one. There, on TV! Look at that punk standing over the empty crib, a picture of the baby tucked in a blanket. He smiles at the camera when a reporter asks if he's involved. You know what he did then?"

Wild Bill continued his rant before Norm could answer.

"He winks at the fucking camera and says, 'do I look like a bad guy to you?' I don't like that kid. He smells bad to me. Kids having kids. She's only fifteen and looks twelve."

Like a gun, he pointed his forefinger and thumb at Norm.

"Get me some dirt on this guy, before the media makes him into some kind of hero. The asshole was drunk and passed out when the kid went missing."

Norm went downstairs, checked in with his boss in the Drug Squad, and brought him up to date on Wild Bill's request.

S/Sgt. Hayes shook his head and responded.

"I saw the news. No wonder Clark blew a gasket. The American media? That's crazy."

Norm nodded in agreement.

"Did we get another car to replace the Toyota?"

"No, see if Clark's got one for you or call the garage to see what they've got. We need the other two vehicles here."

"Ten-Four. I gotta make some calls and get on this baby thing before Wild Bill goes postal."

Hayes smiled.

"Keep me in the loop, Norm."

Five

Reaching Out

Roger Storey was a west-ender, well known to police and criminals alike. His misspent youth had him in and out of jail for every crime but homicide. Old age brought him bad health and a newfound belief in god. He hoped to eke out a few more years on earth.

Norm had busted Roger for dealing crack and in his attempt to avoid incarceration he became Norm's informant. He said he was too old to go back to jail and only sold drugs to supplement his government income.

Storey told Norm he didn't smoke crack, only weed for medicinal purposes. He was disappointed with his nephew, Jeffrey, who'd become addicted to rock cocaine. Roger gave Norm the name of Jeffrey's dealer, thinking the kid might stop using if he lost his source. Roger moved him into his place hoping to straighten him out. Using Storey's information, Norm busted Jeffrey's dealer.

Additional information from Roger resulted in enough arrests and drug seizures to work his patch (trade off his criminal charges), and to make a few bucks via Crime-Stoppers. Storey was happy he'd found a new way to supplement his income.

Norm dropped a dime to Roger and exchanged 'hellos' and 'how are yas'. He asked if they could meet, but Storey said he couldn't get out for a few hours. He took the cordless phone outside so he could speak freely.

Strom asked, "Have you seen the TV news?"

"Yeah, my nephew's all geeked up about it. He works with Brewer."

"No shit. Where?"

"TJ's Body Shop; it's around the corner, on Sandwich. He called me and told me to turn on the tube. Kenny didn't show up for work and he's all over the news."

"Do you know the kid?"

Roger hacked, it sounded as if he'd coughed up a lung.

"No, but I drank with his old man at the Chip. Never had much use for him, but he liked to throw his money around on cheque day."

"Can you put a bug in Jeffrey's ear and see what else he knows, or maybe heard at work? You know how nobody talks to the cops in your neighbourhood. Remind him he owes me for getting him off that possession charge."

"He only knows I called in a favour. Jeffrey doesn't know who you are or anything about our relationship, but I'll talk to him."

"Good, it's smart keeping our connection just between us. I've seen other guys get burned."

"I hear ya, I'll call if I hear anything."

Norm hung up. He flipped to the back page of his note book and found Jennifer Desjardin's number. She was an informant who lived in the west end and called him from time to time with information that was nice to know, instead of the need to know stuff that was required to obtain search warrants or provide enough grounds for an arrest.

Her phone rang five times, then the answering machine clicked on. Norm was about to leave a message when Jennifer picked up. She was out of breath.

"I'm here...hello!"

"Jennifer, its Norm Strom. Did I catch you at a bad time?"

"No, I just came up from the laundry room and ran in from the hall when I heard the phone ringing. How are you, Norm?"

"I'm good. Have you seen the news today about the missing baby?"

"No, but another woman told me about it while we were in the basement. That's terrible. They live right down the street from here."

Norm took a sip of Pepsi and cleared his throat. "Do you still live in the apartment on Chippewa at Bloomfield?"

"Still here. It works for me, and I'm close to my mom. I check on her every day. She doesn't get out anymore, can hardly walk with her bad hip. They want to replace it, but she says she's too old. I said..."

He cut her off, knowing she'd babble on for an hour.

"Do you know the couple with the missing baby?"

"No, but maybe you should talk to Margie."

"Margie?"

"She's on the third floor. Everyone calls her the doll lady. She has hundreds of them and says she's going to have her own baby someday. Margie even pretends she's pregnant or that she has a baby. She pushes her dolls around in a stroller."

"Wow. Do you think she's capable of kidnapping?"

"Beats me. I'm friendly to her and say hi, but I make excuses to get away from her cause she likes to talk forever. My mother says I should..."

Norm cut her off again.

"Do you know her last name or what apartment she's in?"

"Three something...I can go look and call you back."

"That would be great. Can you punch the apartment number in when you call my pager? I'm going to be busy tracking down some other people and I might not be able to get to the phone."

"I can do that. Stop by if you're in the neighbourhood, I made those chocolate chip cookies you like."

"Thanks, Jen. I gotta go."

Six

Seconded

Jolene Lockwood was beside herself. She couldn't stop crying and hadn't eaten since before Shay went missing. She'd managed to wash the smeared mascara from her face, but swollen eyes gave her the appearance of a boxer who'd lost a fight. She blamed Kenny but didn't say any more about it to him. She was afraid he might harm her.

He seemed genuinely upset at times, but angrier more than anything else. He cursed the cops for not doing their jobs, the neighbors for being nosy, and her for having the baby in the first place. The only people he didn't complain about were the reporters who pestered him for updates. Kenny liked the attention.

The garage man said there were no cars available. Norm called Wild Bill and told him he had a couple leads to follow up on, but no wheels to use.

"You can have mine; I'm not going anywhere. Come pick up the keys and your partner."

"Partner?"

"Bingham. I called him in on his day off. My lead crew's stuck in high court with a jury trial. Nobody's going home tonight. Black and Simms are running the canvass and getting statements. Consider yourself seconded to CIB."

He hung up before Norm could respond. He did that a lot.

Bingham was a golden boy who was junior to him in seniority, but always one step up on the company ladder. They'd recently promoted him to Detective, although he had no investigative experience. Norm had the prerequisite courses and training but was passed over. It was political and he had no vote or say in the matter.

Attired in a double-breasted navy-blue suit, David Bingham stood beside Clarke's desk looking serious and lost at the same time. He broke eye contact with Wild Bill just long enough to size up Norm, clad in a black Chicago Bulls tee shirt, jeans and Nikes. Bingham smirked.

The Staff Sergeant tossed Norm his car keys.

"Check out your leads, then hook up with Black and Simms. They got a name, Neil Shipley; the mother's ex-boyfriend. Records say your guys busted him with drugs."

He surveyed Bingham's clothes.

"You'll be able to relate to him better than my guys in their fancy suits."

"I remember him—wasn't much of a talker, but it was a small amount of weed and he knew he'd only get a slap on the wrist."

Clarke eyed his new Detective again.

"Bingham, you got any street clothes? Nobody on the west side's gonna talk to you in that suit."

Norm grinned. It wasn't that he didn't like the guy. They'd worked and partied together when they were on the same patrol shift. Maybe it was jealousy. It was difficult to teach the job to newbies, and then watch them pass you by on the promotional list. Bingham had been a good street cop and would probably make a good Detective, once he learned the ropes.

Unbelievable, Norm thought, as Bing folded his six-foot-four athletic frame into the car. He'd changed into his dirty baseball uniform. Norm laughed, shook his head.

"Did Wild Bill see that?"

"No, I was playing ball when he called me in. The suit was in my locker."

"He said street clothes, not a dirty ball uniform."

The new Detective scrunched his face.

"At least I didn't wear my spikes. We won, by the way."

Norm drove south from the police station.

"We'll stop at your place first, so you can change your clothes again."

"Okay, but you're going the wrong way."

"What? Aren't you in South Windsor?"

"Janice and the kids are, I'm renting a shoebox in Walkerville."

Norm bit his lower lip.

"Sorry to hear that, Bing. Guess the guys were right when they said you were crazy for buying that giant engagement ring. Someone said that thing set you back ten grand."

"Yeah, but she was good breeding stock. My boy's gonna be a pro athlete someday. You should see him skate."

Norm grinned, turned east.

"Kids. Better you than me, being DINKs means Sandra and I can spend all our money on us."

"DINKs?"

"Double Income, No Kids. These days most of our cash is going into the money pit."

Bing cracked a smile. "We had some great parties in that mansion...the good old days."

Norm nodded in agreement.

"We surely did. Too bad we all got transferred or promoted."

He eyed Bing.

"Well, at least some of us did."

"I thought I lucked out getting assigned to Clarke's platoon, but it feels like my first week in high school."

"You're playing with the big boys now. Too bad you're the odd man in the unit, with no regular partner to teach you the ropes and watch your back."

"Guess I got one now, hey Storm?"

"Fuck you! First, I teach your rookie ass on the street, and now I gotta show ya how to be a Dick? You'll probably be my boss next."

He punched Norm's arm.

"Your day will come Storm. It's only because I aced the exam."

"You mean you cheated, like the other clowns who moved ahead of me on the list."

Bing rolled his eyes and turned his head to hide the grin.

Back in the car, after trading his ball uniform for a pair of wrinkled jeans and a tee shirt, he turned to Norm.

"So, what's our agenda?"

He regarded the change in clothes.

"Pull those out of the hamper?"

Bing shrugged.

"Gimme a break...no more laundry bitch."

"First stop is on Chippewa. I have a friend who lives there and says there's a woman in the building with a thing for babies. A nutcase who has a bunch of dolls and pretends they're real newborns."

Norm checked his pager.

"She was supposed to send me the apartment number."

"She?"

"Don't get too excited, unless you're looking for a cum-dumpster, now that you're single. She's a good baker, makes awesome pies and cookies."

"Works for me, I haven't eaten all day. Any other leads?"

"I got a buddy whose nephew works with the grieving father. And Clarke says Black and Simms have the name of an ex-boyfriend who I've busted before."

He caught Bing with his peripheral vision. He scribbled notes while Norm filled him in and drove across town. The man could have been a poster boy for the police. Tall, blonde and handsome, with cool blue eyes and a chiseled chin. His athletic build showed through his clothes.

Norm stopped in front of Jennifer Desjardin's apartment building.

"This is it. We're looking for a chick named Margie, who lives on the third floor."

They entered the foyer and browsed the list of tenants and buzzers. There was no Margie listed, most of the labels simply read, 'occupied.' Bing tugged on the locked door.

"Why aren't they required to display their names? Would make our job easier."

"I guess Welfare folks are entitled to privacy too." He buzzed #604.

A crackly female voice answered.

"C'mon in, Norm, I've got fresh baked goods."

Seven

Apple Pie

Situated in the middle of the west side housing projects, Jennifer Desjardins lived in a geared-to-income apartment building. Considering the other homes in the neighbourhood, her building was in good repair. She was standing in the hall with her door open, when the cops got off the elevator. The smell of fresh baked goods wafted down the hall.

"Hey, Norm, who's your handsome friend? I got Margie's last name and apartment number, she..."

"Hi, Jen. Maybe we should talk inside your apartment."

She nodded in acknowledgement, then Strom and Bingham followed her into the open concept living room/dining room. Bing eyed the freshly baked pie on the table. Forks and plates and napkins were set on placemats, waiting to be used.

"Do you guys want ice cream with your apple pie. I have French Vanilla or Pralines and Cream?"

Bing looked like a kid on Christmas morning, anxious to tear open his presents. Norm didn't need the calories. He told himself he didn't want to insult the host, and he knew Jen's baking was good. He glanced at Bing whose lips were pressed together, probably to prevent himself from drooling.

"Whatever you have open will be fine, Jen."

"Okay, I'll give you a scoop of each, you're both big guys." She blushed and smiled at Bing.

Norm introduced them. "This is Detective Bingham. Bing, meet Jennifer Desjardins."

"It's nice to meet you, Detective."

She turned and went to the kitchen freezer. His head on a swivel, Bing checked out the apartment. He nodded his approval to Norm. Both cops appreciated her clean and tidy unit. They saw too many dirty and cockroach infested homes in this neighborhood. Like a magnet, the pie drew Bing to the table. They sat. Jen returned with two tubs of ice cream.

"I've got Pepsi for you, Norm. What would you like to drink, Detective Bingham?"

"A glass of milk would be great, if you have some?"

"Coming right up. Go ahead and cut yourselves a slice, don't be shy."

Bingham had his knife into the crust before she could finish her sentence.

"Bing, everyone calls me Bing."

Her coconut-brown eyes widened. She brushed a loose strand of the same color hair off her forehead. Jen wasn't a typical west-end welfare chick. A bit on the frumpy side, she was the kind of woman who'd look like JayLo after a six pack of beer. In her forties, she was probably a six out of ten when she was half that age.

"Any leads on Shay, Norm?"

Both men had their mouths full of pie and ice cream. Norm took a swig of pop to help him swallow and answered the question.

"Who?"

"The missing baby, Shay. Oh, before I forget, I spoke to Margie and asked for her last name. She's below me, in apartment 304. It's Margie Belanger."

"You asked for her last name, didn't she think that was unusual?"

"I told her I was on the building's social committee and we were collecting names and interests from all the tenants."

Bing barely glanced up from his plate. Norm forked some ice cream onto a chunk of pie.

"Pretty slick, Jen, you should be a Detective."

She let out a rapid-fire ha-ha-ha laugh, her eyes were fixed on Bing.

"Margie's always home if you want to talk to her."

Jen saw that Bing had finished his pie.

"Did you like it? Help yourself to some more."

He contemplated for about two seconds.

"It's delicious, Jen, maybe just another little piece."

She carved out another generous slab. Norm washed down his last bite with the pop.

"I appreciate you getting Margie's name and number. Did you talk to her inside her apartment?"

"Not really, she stood in the doorway and didn't invite me in. I couldn't tell if there was a real baby in there. Do you think she took Shay?"

"I don't know. We'll check it out when Bing's done filling his face."

He eyed the younger detective and motioned with his fingers for him to wipe a glob of ice cream from the corner of his mouth.

Jennifer fell into a tirade about weirdoes like Margie, drug dealers in the neighbourhood, and the building manager who continually hit on her. After another glance from Norm, Bing caught on that it was time to go. Their plates clean, and stomachs full, they thanked their host and headed for the door.

The Detectives took the three flights of stairs down for exercise, then knocked on the door of apartment #304.

Eight

Doll House

The woman who answered the door gawked at the two Detectives. They produced their police ID and Bingham asked the woman if she was Marjorie Belanger. She nodded in affirmation but stayed behind the door.

Strom asked, "Can we come in and talk to you?"

Belanger wore a white cotton sweat suit. Her curly hair and fuzzy socks were jet black. A chess board popped into Norm's mind.

"My baby's sleeping, what do you want?"

As if on cue, a baby cried out from inside the apartment. Like a hockey player on a breakaway, Bing charged through the opening, almost knocking Margie over. Norm followed him into the apartment and stepped in front of the woman before she caught up to his partner. She danced from side to side, trying to step around the cop twice her size.

Agitated, she got loud.

"What are you doing? You can't barge in here like this. I have to check on my baby."

"Relax, Margie, we're looking for a missing baby. We want to make sure yours is okay."

Her eyes widened and darted wildly around the room. She made another attempt to out flank Norm.

"That's my baby in there! You're looking for baby Shay. She's not here."

Bing appeared in the bedroom doorway. He had a crying doll by the scruff of its neck in one hand and a baby blanket in the other. Rolling his eyes, he shook his head.

"Storm, you gotta check this out."

Margie yelled at Bing, "What are you doing? You can't hold her like that. You're gonna hurt Melanie!"

Norm let her pass. She took the doll from Bing, wrapped it in the blanket, and cradled it in her arms. He stepped around her and looked in the bedroom. It was decorated as a nursery, complete with a crib and change table. Dozens of other dolls lined shelves on the walls, the dresser, bed and headboard. Margie sang a lullaby.

Bing didn't say a word. The expression on his face said he'd seen enough, and it was time to go. Focussed on her baby, Margie ignored them. They left without another word.

Back in the car, Bing spoke first.

"Holy fuck; just when you think you've seen it all."

"Yeah, that's one for the memoirs. Let's go meet Black and Simms, see what they've heard about Shipley."

"Who?"

"Neil Shipley, the grieving mommy's ex-boyfriend. They got some info from the canvass. Wild Bill wants us to interview him."

The four Detectives met at the Tim Horton's on Huron Church and Totten. Black and Simms reviewed canvass sheets and caught up on their notes. They saw Strom and Bingham walk in the door, Simms eyeballed their attire, mumbled something about the neighborhood. Black greeted them, "What are you two defectives up too?"

Norm answered. "Nice suit, Black, Salvation Army?"

The pin stripes matched the grey that streaked his slicked black hair and cop mustache.

Simms added his two cents.

"A Narc and a rookie Dick, who's teaching who?"

He had a square and balding head. His hair resembled a Chia Pet and his beard looked as if it was pruned with hedge trimmers.

Norm forced a chuckle that sounded more like a grunt. He and Bing sat at the table with the pair of Detectives.

"Wild Bill said Neil Shipley came up on your radar during the canvass. He wants us to take a crack at him."

Simms spoke. "And why would our Staff Sergeant want you two questioning our person of interest?"

"Probably cuz I busted him for possession. Guess he thinks we bonded. Why don't you call your boss and ask him."

Black shook his head, didn't bother to look up from his notebook. Simms brushed cookie crumbs off the table with the back of his hand and answered.

"The word on the street is that Shipley thinks the missing baby is his. He was banging Jolene before that shithead she lives with now. Guess there was some confusion because they were both doing her at the same time."

"She got around?"

"You could say that. They call her 'Jolene the blowjob queen'."

Norm winced, glanced at Bing.

"Maybe she should have swallowed. We'd have one less welfare case to worry about."

Black flipped through the pages in his notebook.

"Guess you can have a go at Shipley since Wild Bill says so. The boy lives with his mommy at 9418 Brock Street, close to the county jail. Good for visitation."

Bing jotted down Shipley's address. Norm stood up.

Simms asked, "What, no donuts?"

Bing grinned and rubbed his belly.

"One of Norm's west end rats filled us up with apple pie and ice cream."

"And you're still alive? You actually ate something in that neighbourhood."

Norm scoffed.

"Us Narcs live dangerously. Maybe I'll bring you some of her chocolate chip cookies next time."

Black and Simms shook their heads in unison. Strom and Bingham left the table and headed for the door.

Norm parked the car two houses south of Shipley's address on Brock.

Bing commented, "There's a spot right out front."

"I don't want them to see us coming. Surprise is more fun."

Norm led the way, across a neighbour's lawn, then up the front porch steps at 9418. All the curtains were drawn, and the inside door was closed. There was no view inside. The door was positioned near the left corner of the brick house. Norm leaned over the railing and peeked into the side yard.

A man wearing a black tee shirt and jeans was hunched over at the back corner of the house, tending to a four-foot marihuana plant. Before Norm could pull his head back, the guy turned and made eye contact. It was Shipley. He ran.

Nine

Dumpster Diving

Bing vaulted the porch railing and sprinted into the back yard. By the time Norm got back into the car and drove around to the next street, all he saw was Shipley's blonde ponytail when he disappeared into a cedar hedge. He drove to the next street. A police cruiser was parked near the blue dumpster at the back of the corner store, but there were no cops in sight.

Thinking they'd joined in the chase, Norm circled the block and stopped in front of a house where he heard a dog barking. Bing appeared from between two houses. He was limping and rubbing his elbow. When he got to the car, he was slick with sweat, had a scuffed forearm, and grass stains on one pant leg.

Norm asked, "You alright? You wipe out?"

"Yeah, I took a corner in third gear, but forgot I wasn't wearing my cleats."

"You see Shipley or the other cops?"

Bing used his forearm to wipe sweat from his brow.

"He disappeared into thin air. What cops are you talking about?"

He got into the car, cranked up the air conditioning, then reached for the radio.

"I already called it in. There's a cruiser around the corner, I thought they'd joined you in the chase."

Bing checked his elbow.

"You want a Band-Aid for your booboo?"

"I didn't see any other cops. I lost sight of Shipley when I wiped out. He was heading this way; he didn't pop out here?"

"Nope."

Norm circled back around the block. The dispatcher asked for their status. He reported the suspect was at large, wanted for cultivation and possession of a narcotic. A cop in fatigues, stood near the cruiser at the corner store. It was Jesse, Norm's best friend. They pulled up alongside him.

Jesse leaned in Norm's window, sighed.

Norm spoke first.

"Hey, brother, what are you...what the fuck is that smell? You step in dog shit?"

He pointed toward the garbage bin. Another head popped up inside the container.

"Wild Bill's got ESU (Emergency Services Unit) checking dumpsters for the missing baby."

He wiped his face with a wad of napkins he'd pulled from his pocket.

"What are you doing around here, not busting dopers today?"

"Funny you should ask. Did you see a guy in a black tee shirt and blonde ponytail run by here?"

Jesse dabbed sweat from the back of his neck.

"You got any napkins in your nice air-conditioned car?"

Bing searched the glove box, but he'd used the last one for himself.

Norm shrugged.

"Guess not."

Jesse raised his eyebrows. The whole unit is on garbage patrol. He nodded toward his partner who was climbing out of the bin.

"We're dumpster divers. Another crew is checking alleys, and some guys are at the city landfill checking what comes out of the garbage trucks."

Norm commented. "It's not just a job, it's an adventure."

"Fuck!" Jesse's partner yelled and stomped his feet. He kicked the side of the bin and swatted his pant legs. They were covered in maggots.

Norm and Bing broke out in laughter.

Jesse stepped back and checked himself for bugs.

"We were told that someone saw Brewer leave his house with a garbage bag on the night the baby went missing. A witness thought he left in a car."

Bing asked, "He has wheels?"

"Not that we know of, but we have to check every stinking garbage can on the west side."

Norm eyed Jesse.

"You get a description of the car?"

"Not much...dark coloured two-door, maybe an older model Chevy. Who were you guys chasing?"

Norm answered. "Neil Shipley. Word is he thinks baby Shay is his kid. Guess Jolene, the BJ Queen, was doing him and Brewer at the same time. We went to question him, but he bolted when we caught him admiring his pot plant. Does Wild Bill think Brewer killed the baby?"

"Everyone thinks that. Last time we drove by the house he and the skank were on the front porch talking to a news crew. He was spouting off and pointed at us. She was sitting on the steps balling her eyes out, a female reporter had an arm around her. They sure love the limelight."

Another police cruiser drove by. The passenger shrugged and lifted his hands in the air. They hadn't seen Shipley either.

Jesse tapped on the roof of Norm's car.

"Looks like you're having as much luck as we are today. Think your doper's hiding out in the hood?"

Norm nodded.

"Yeah, probably crawled under a rock or is enjoying a cold beer with one of his homies."

He put the car in gear.

"Catch ya later, brother, we're gonna go do some real police work. Enjoy your dumpster diving."

Jesse fluffed his auburn hair as if he was checking for more bugs. He stepped away from the car and called out to them. "Assholes."

Bing adjusted the air vent, aimed it at his face.

"So, what are we gonna do about Shipley?"

Norm drove in the direction of his house.

"Well, first we're gonna scoop that plant of his, and anything else illegal that might be in plain view."

"We can do that?"

"What's he gonna do...call the cops and say someone stole his marihuana plant?"

Bing smiled, rubbed his sore elbow.

Norm frowned; the garden soil was loose in a bare spot where the plant had been.

"Shit!" Bing shouted.

"Do you think he came back and took it?"

Before Norm could answer, a woman spoke up.

"Who are ya and what are ya doin in my yard?"

The pale, white-haired woman appeared from the back door of the house. She possessed the features of an albino. Norm pointed to the badge on his belt.

"Police, we're looking for your son, Neil."

"Not home. Why dint you knock on the door like cops are sposed to?" Unafraid, she advanced on the two Detectives.

Twice her size, Bing took a step back. Norm put a hand up.

"We're sorry for the intrusion, ma'am. We came to talk to Neil, but he ran when he saw us...probably because of the marihuana plant that was here in the garden."

He pointed to the barren spot.

The woman swivelled her head.

"No plants like that round here. Neil's a good boy. What ya want him for?"

"We wanted to question him about his relationship with Jolene Lockwood and her missing baby."

She spit at Norm's feet.

"That whore? Told Neil she was no good. White trash, like her mother."

Norm glanced down at his shoes, worried they'd been spat on.

"We were told that Neil thinks the baby is his."

"Just to prove he's a man...that his gun don't shoot blanks an all that macho crap. Neil wouldn't know what to do with a kid and I sure as hell don't need another one round here. Ya leavin' now?"

Bing was already backing away. Norm nodded.

"Sorry to bother you, ma'am. We're just doing our jobs."

"Fucking cops. Do it somewheres else."

Ten

Kiddie Diddlers

Norm pointed the car toward the Detroit River.
Bing winced and rubbed his elbow for the fifteenth time.
"What now? Can you believe that old bitch, Storm?"
"Which part? There never was a weed plant in the yard, Neil's a good boy, or Jolene's a skanky whore?"
"I used to think people were honest for the most part. Now I don't know. Everybody lies to us all the time. Hey, can we get something to drink? I want to clean my elbow too, before it gets infected."
Norm scoffed.
"Sorry, that wasn't meant for you. It was for west-enders in general, and their love of cops and mankind. You want to swing by an ER, have a nurse look at that?"
"Nah, just something cold to drink and some more napkins for the blood and sweat. Can it get any friggen hotter?"
They drove by TJ's Auto on Sandwich Street. Norm sucked in his lower lip.
"Shit, they're closed. I was hoping to talk to someone there."
Bing glanced at the shop, then turned his gaze to the variety store up the block.
"It's after five, Norm, most people only work eight-hour days. Think we'll be late tonight?"
"Is water wet? Wild Bill's on the case and you know what he likes to say?"
"No, what?"
"Solve no crime before overtime. Why, you got a date or something?"
"My son's playing ball. I never missed a game before I transferred to CIB."

Norm clucked.

"You're in the big leagues now and on Wild Bill's team. Get used to it, man."

They pulled into the parking lot at the corner store. Bing moaned.

"I never get to see my kids anymore. I'm supposed to have shared custody."

He reached for the door handle once the car came to a stop.

"Just think of all the cash your making. It'll pay for their college education. Hey, grab me a Pepsi and Kit Kat bar?"

Bing stepped out and replied before the door closed.

"I was hoping my boy makes the big leagues, to supplement my retirement."

Norm's pager vibrated. The number displayed belonged to the CIB office. He got out to use the pay phone in front of the store. There was nothing but a wire dangling where the receiver should have been. He went into the store.

Bing was at the cash register.

"I got your sugar fix."

"Gotta call in, office paged me. Someone destroyed the phone outside."

He asked the attendant to use his landline.

"Sure, officer, that payphone's been like that for months. They don't fix it anymore cuz it just gets broke the next day." The clerk shrugged.

Bing asked for the keys while Norm made the phone call. The secretary told him that S/Sgt. Clarke was holding a briefing in forty-five minutes and he wanted everyone there. When Norm got back in the car Bing had the air cranked.

"Did you get some Band-Aids?"

"No. I'll survive. What's up?"

"You can clean up back at the barn. Team meeting, Wild Bill's called everyone in."

The CIB office looked like a police convention. Detectives and constables in plain clothes and in uniform sat on chairs and desks and stood against the walls. Norm recognized most faces, except for a few rookies. The force was large, but small enough to know almost everyone.

Officers from the Special Investigations Branch were in the mix. Their mandate was liquor and morality, as well as sex offences. Norm wondered if there were any cops left on the street.

Staff Sergeant Clarke stood up behind his desk and addressed the room.

"Listen up. I know a lot of you have been at it all day, but it will be dark soon, and the end of our first forty-eight hours. You know what that means. Time is running out.

Those of you with sex offender lists will be teaming up with SIB to knock on doors. You'll check on every known pervert in the city, starting with those on the west side. So, go and hit the streets."

About half the cops left the room. Those that remained looked worn and tired. Suits were wrinkled, shirtsleeves rolled up, uniforms soiled. The smell of sweat and ripe garbage fouled the air. Jesse and three others on his team looked like they'd lost a mud wrestling match.

The Staff Inspector in charge of Investigations stood near his office door. He donned the only fresh-looking face in the room.

Wild Bill spoke again.

"Okay, let's hear what we got people. We'll go around the room. Black, Simms?"

Black replied. "Yes, sir. The canvass hasn't given us much more than you already know...the tip about Brewer with the garbage bag and car. We had additional info on Neil Shipley, but it seems someone lost him."

Clarke cut in. "Normie, what happened out there?"

"Sorry, Staff, he bolted when saw us at his house. He was tending to a pot plant at the time."

Wild Bill stuck his baby finger in his right ear, twisted it, and dug for wax. His oval noggin and the two large fleshy appendages on either side of it gave him the appearance of Mr. Potato Head, but no one would ever suggest it out loud.

"I don't care about weed in his garden, what happened to Shipley?"

Bingham answered. "Sorry, boss. I chased him, but he got away. We think one of the neighbours is harbouring him. His mother was home. Said she didn't have much use for Jolene Lockwood or any baby that might have been fathered by Brewer or her son."

"Anything else?"

Norm answered. "We struck out with a crazy woman in the apartments at Bloomfield and Chippewa. She thinks her dolls are real people. One of her neighbours gave her up as a suspect when Shay went missing."

Wild Bill sat down behind his desk, gave a long sigh.

"Anything else? What about that kid you said worked with Brewer at the garage?"

"Uh, yeah. He's the nephew of one of my CI's. Worked with Brewer at TJ's Auto, but they were closed by the time we got there. There is something else we could follow up on there."

"What's that?"

"A car parked in the lot has the company logo on the door. It looks like the one Brewer might have used. I'm wondering if employees have access to it. Maybe we can ask the business owner?"

Clarke leaned back in his chair, craned his neck and stretched.

"He won't tell us shit. That's Terry Boomer's place. He hates cops. Might have something to do with me busting his nose years ago. Wild Bill sprung forward and folded his hands on the desk.

"Talk to your fink, his nephew, whoever. Find out if Brewer has access to that car. If he does, tow it and have it examined. I'll deal with Boomer later."

He surveyed the remaining strained faces in the room.

"Anyone else?"

Jesse spoke up. "We've checked every alley and dumpster from Brock Street to Prince Road, and from College to Sandwich. We still have two guys at the landfill waiting for the last trucks to come in. Anywhere else you want us to look?"

"Take a walk through the abandoned lots and fields along the river, before it gets dark."

He looked at the west side sergeant.

"Anything to add, Joe?"

"Nothing, Bill. My guys swept the whole neighbourhood on foot. I still have two out there with the Windsor Housing Authority. They're checking empty and abandoned houses. Kids break in and party in them on weekends. Anything you can do about the media? They keep hounding my guys."

"Leave it with me, I'll have to give them a statement before the day is done."

He folded his hands behind his head, surveyed the room once again.

"Thanks, everyone. I know you're tired, but it ain't over yet. Maybe we'll have some luck with the perverts and kiddie diddlers."

Eleven

Nightfall

From Headquarters, they drove west on Riverside Drive, admiring the scenery along the Detroit River. The Motor City showed its best face on the Windsor side of the international border. The reflection of the setting sun in the mirrored windows of the Renaissance Center gave it the appearance of a glass lantern. The last remnants of daylight twinkled on ripples in the water.

Norm was awed by how everything calmed at night; city traffic, people, industry, and the river. Bing stared out his window in silence. The Narc considered his next move, he couldn't get in touch with Roger Storey or his nephew.

They headed for TJ's Auto, hoping the company's courtesy car was still parked on the lot there. Not knowing if it would help further the case, Norm figured it couldn't hurt to have a closer look at it. He brought along a Polaroid camera, thinking he'd use a photo of the car to show the witness.

The burgundy Impala was parked in TJ's lot, behind two wrecked cars that were awaiting repairs. Norm stopped in front of the suspect vehicle, with the headlights illuminating it. It sported the company's logo they'd seen earlier in the day. Bing joined him as he walked around the car.

"What are we looking for, Storm?"

"Something...anything. We don't know for sure if Brewer used this car, or if he's got anything to do with his daughter's disappearance."

"Really? You gotta be the only one thinking that."

Norm put his face to a window and peered into the Impala.

"Don't get me wrong, I think he's good for it too, but we're a long way from being able to prove it. He's the kind of asshole that everyone wants to be guilty. He looks like...hey, Bing, what do you make of that?"

He joined Norm at the rear passenger window.

"What are you looking at?"

Norm stabbed the glass with his finger.

"On the floor, there. Is that what I think it is? You got a flashlight?"

"In the glove box, hang on a sec."

Bing returned a moment later and aimed the light at the floor of the back seat. A small object was partially concealed under the front seat.

"Holy shit, Storm, that's a baby pacifier."

He tried the passenger door handle, but it was locked. "That's what I thought. I'm gonna grab the camera, see if we can get a picture."

The excitement in Bing's voice was obvious.

"Why don't we just tow the car like the boss said?"

Norm thought about it while he retrieved the camera. He returned and placed the camera against the window.

"I wonder if the flash will bounce off the glass."

They were interrupted by the sound of tires on gravel. Bright headlights temporarily blinded the two cops. A pickup truck stopped inches short of their unmarked police vehicle, and a man jumped out of the driver's door wielding a tire iron.

He shouted, "What the fuck do you think you're doing?"

Bing aimed his flashlight at the man's face. He was unshaven and his hair was slicked back, tied in a ponytail.

He edged forward.

"Get that fucking light out of my face; you're trespassing."

Norm responded. "Windsor Police. Come any closer with that tire iron and we will shoot you."

Bing had a hand on his gun.

"You're on my property. You got a warrant?"

"Take it easy, sir. Who are you?"

The man held the weapon at his side.

"I own this place and you got no business here unless you got a warrant."

Norm took a step toward the man.

"We're looking for a missing baby."

"I don't care what you're looking for, I want you off my property. NOW!"

Remembering what Clarke had said about TJ, Norm gave Bing a glance, then put a hand up.

"Alright, sir, we're leaving. Do you mind if we come back in the morning and talk to your employees?"

"Sure. Just tell me what time so I can have my lawyer here. On second thought, maybe you should call him first. Paul Rivait...I'm sure you've heard of him."

The Detectives made their way back to their car. TJ got back into his truck, but he didn't move until they exited the driveway.

"Do you believe that asshole, Storm, what do we do now? Couldn't we arrest him for obstruction?"

Norm drove toward the variety store down the street.

"On his own property? He was right about us trespassing."

"But we're investigating..."

"Investigating what? We don't' even have a crime until we find a body. It's only a missing person investigation right now." Norm pulled over down the road.

Bing was puzzled.

"What are you doing?"

"I'm going to call Wild Bill, and then my CI. He paged me during our standoff. I want you to walk along that hedgerow back there and find a spot where you can keep an eye on the car. Make sure TJ doesn't mess with it. I doubt he knows about the pacifier in the back seat or even if Brewer used the vehicle."

Bing looked back at the body shop, TJ's headlights were still visible.

"Sounds like a plan. I'll take the radio, just in case."

"I'll be down the street at the variety store, I'm gonna use their phone and see what the boss wants to do. He can apply for a warrant if he wants us to yank the car."

Bing got out of the car and headed for the bushes. Norm drove to the store, keeping an eye on Bing in the rear-view mirror. The daytime clerk was still behind the counter, it appeared he worked the same long hours that they did. He nodded when Norm asked for the phone. He called Wild Bill; it went directly to his desk.

"Boss, Norm here. We've got a problem."

Twelve

Snagged

Two of Joe Major's favourite things in life were Saturday mornings and fishing. After a week of hoisting sheets of drywall twice his size, and inhaling clouds of compound dust, he looked forward to sitting at the edge of the Detroit River where he watched Lake Huron's bounty carried to Lake Erie.

Programmed from years of rising early in the morning, he pulled into the field off Russell Street, shortly after sunup. It was one of his favorite fishing holes. Joe once landed a three-foot Muskie there. He had to release it because it was too small to legally keep.

It was said that Sturgeon also ran the deep trench that had been dredged to allow huge lake freighters passage. He only dreamed of such a catch.

His Irish setter, Red, sat in the passenger seat. The dog always got antsy when they neared the water. Joe held up a hand to the dog and gave the command, 'Stay.' He got out of the van and eyed Red, who sat still, waiting anxiously.

When he snapped his fingers, Red leaped from the vehicle, barely touching the driver's seat on the way out. The dog put his nose to work in the long grass, still damp with morning dew.

Joe removed his rod, tackle, chair, and lunch pail from the back of his van. Red led the way, scouting the path to their perch. At the river's edge, he flipped his seat open and put his gear down beside it. He gazed at the city of Detroit across the river, it appeared hospitable in the early morning light.

He'd heard yellow lake perch were running just off shore. Joe admired the view, twisted and stretched his neck to get the kinks out. An empty beer can in the grass caught his eye. He hated litter.

Red had his two front paws in the water, his nose to the wind. Joe snapped his fingers, pointed, and gave his dog a command.

"Fetch!"

Red eyed the spot, then charged into the grass. He retrieved the crumpled aluminum and dropped it at Joe's side. He rubbed and patted the dog's head, then praised him.

"Good Boy."

He retrieved a thermos from his lunch box and poured himself a coffee. Joe took a sip, gazed across the river, and sighed. Life was good. He took the carton of worms from his lunchbox, thought about it for a second, and then grabbed a cookie. The rustling sound brought Red to Joe's side. He retrieved a dog cookie from his pocket and handed his buddy a treat.

A fat night crawler squirmed and tried to escape Joe's grasp when he pierced its skin to bait the hook on his fishing line. Red wandered off, checking the brush along the shoreline. The dog never wandered too far. Joe tossed his line into the river and tightened the slack. He sat back, grabbed the coffee, sipped, and sighed.

Time drifted by; the warmth of the sun dried any dew that remained on the grass. The crisp blue sky was evidence of a front that moved in overnight. The cooler air was a nice change from the recent humid weather.

Joe soaked his oatmeal cookie in his coffee. He thought he'd felt a nibble on his line, pulled it in, and checked the bait. Surprised that nobody else was there fishing on that beautiful morning, Joe smiled at the solitude.

The line was returned to the water. He felt the sun's heat on the back of his neck and raised his collar. Red growled. He tore at the soil with his paws. Joe whistled and called his name, but the dog continued to growl and dig. Joe secured the rod in his chair and went to check on his buddy.

The dog tugged on something that was buried in the weeds. The earth had been disturbed, as though someone had been digging there. Joe grabbed Red's collar and pulled him back. He saw something protruding from the dirt.

He bent down for a closer look and saw a tiny hand. A knot formed in his stomach. He used the toe of his shoe to move the soil. The hand was black, its fingers curled.

Another prod with his shoe exposed an arm. It was covered in fur. Using a napkin from his pocket, Joe grabbed hold and gave the arm a tug. It was a dead racoon. Red tried to get closer for a nasal appraisal, but Joe held the dog back.

He carried the animal back to his chair where he stuffed it in the garbage bag. Joe always brought a large bag with him for the litter that others left behind.

Red stood guard by the bag. Then he barked. Something he did whenever Joe hooked a fish. Joe looked at his line and sure enough, the rod was bent in half. He grabbed hold and tried to reel it in. He knew the feel of a snag.

"Damn it, Red, this one's on you."

Joe shrugged. It wasn't a big deal, maybe a buck's worth of bait and tackle if the line broke.

He pulled to the left, and then to the right. The line moved as he reeled it in slowly. His hook had caught on something. A green plastic bag broke the water's surface and Joe continued to pull it in. It drifted near shore and he saw it was a garbage bag; more litter.

Red stood at the water's edge, whimpering.

Joe reached down and pulled the bag from the water. The dog sniffed and pawed it. He scolded the dog.

"Get back Red. It's only garbage."

The dog managed to tear the bag open before Joe could push him back. A small foot appeared. The knot in his stomach returned.

Thirteen

Baby Shay

Norm stood on the crest of a hill, gazed down at the valley and river below. He waited for the right gust of wind, then reached out and lifted off. With the open sky at his back, he surfed the air. Tilting his arms and body one way or the other, he caught the wind like a boat's mainsail. He soared over the water. The pleasure craft and fishing boats below resembled toys bobbing in a bath tub.

He lost altitude, feared a water landing and turned back inland. The ground rushed up at him until his feet found terra firma. Someone shouted his name and pointed to a phone booth. His eyelids like heavy curtains, Norm pulled them open and saw his wife standing over him with the cordless in hand.

The sandman had done a number on him, it was as if he'd awoken from the dead. His lips were dry as unbuttered popcorn, his tongue stuck to the roof of his mouth.

He worked to form a sentence.

"Huh, wuz the matter? Snot time to get up."

Sandra answered. "It is now. Staff Sergeant Clarke's on the phone."

Norm sat up, tried to kick-start his brain. She handed him the phone. He forced saliva from his throat into his mouth and answered the call.

"Ha-hello."

"Normie. Drop your cock and grab your socks. We've got a dead baby."

Norm was not a morning person and struggled to comprehend what he'd just heard.

Clarke raised the level of his voice a notch.

"You've got my wheels. Pick me up out back in twenty minutes. Should give you enough time to get your shit together."

Norm tried to do the math in his head, how long it would take him to wake up and drive downtown.

"You got that, Normie, out back in twenty. The media vultures are circling and I'm not ready to give them an update yet."

He'd made it to the bathroom with the phone still pressed to his ear. Norm sat to relieve himself.

"I can be there in half an hour, boss."

"Twenty. See you then."

He looked in the mirror and used his fingers to fluff his hair. Norm had more than most men his age. Job stress got to him another way. He glanced down at his tummy roll, and what was becoming man boobs. He really needed to lose some weight. He splashed warm water on his face.

On the way downstairs he recalled the dream, it was one that recurred from time to time. According to a book he'd read, it had something to do with being at peace or stress-free. That seemed unlikely, considering the case he was presently working and the news he'd just received by phone.

Dressed and in the kitchen thinking about food, Norm eyed his dog, Brandy. She was at Sandra's feet, waiting for her breakfast or something to fall off the counter. He couldn't recall if he'd kissed his wife and petted the dog, or vice-versa when he'd gotten home only a few hours earlier.

Clarke told him and Bing to get some sleep, leaving a uniformed officer to babysit the car at TJ's, while he put together the information required to obtain a search warrant.

Sandra handed her husband a folded paper towel with a toasted blueberry bagel and cream cheese wrapped inside.

"I saw the lawn mower is still out, do you want me to get one of the boys next door to finish for you?"

"Sure. I dunno when I'll get to it. I gotta fly. Wild Bill's in a mood."

He headed for door, Brandy at his heels. Norm grabbed a Pepsi from the beer fridge on the way out. Sandra was there when he closed the door. She kissed him.

"Nice talking to you. Catch ya later."

He smiled, left the house, and tripped over the cat outside the front door. The name Gretzky seemed appropriate; he was born with a hockey stick-shaped tail. He'd been out whoring all night. After dodging his master's size elevens, he ran into the house for breakfast.

Wild Bill brought Norm up to speed explaining a dead infant had been found in the river. It went without saying who it was. He said the Justice of the Peace wouldn't issue a night-time warrant for the car, and that he was going to re-apply that morning.

Plans changed when a fisherman found the body. Forensics were on the scene. Reporters too. He wasn't very happy about that.

It was a three-ring circus when they got to the vacant lot off Russell Street. Marked and unmarked police cars, media vehicles, the Coroner and body removal people, and lots of gawkers. A young constable lifted the yellow police tape, allowing them into the field.

The Windsor Police boat cruised the shoreline, and the Coast Guard drifted with the current, further off shore. Norm noticed scuba divers on board.

"Are they looking for something in particular, boss?"

Surprised that Wild Bill hadn't called in the Navy too, he nodded toward the river.

"Checking for evidence. They found two abandoned cars on the bottom, so far. Been in there too long to have anything to do with this. Probably stolen."

The group of cops resembled a huddled football team; bunched together where the inner perimeter was sectioned off with crime scene tape. As Clarke approached, they parted like the Red Sea.

The Coroner and two forensic technicians were crouched inside the tape. They hovered over a green garbage bag, split open to reveal its contents. A small baby, bloated and with discoloured skin, lay motionless. One of the techs snapped photographs.

Norm stayed with Clarke, outside the tape. The three men with the body paused and turned in unison at the sound of the S/Sgt's voice.

"Well?"

Nods from the two cops, and a grimace from the Coroner were the only confirmation he needed. Baby Shay was dead. Wild Bill had a private conversation with the Coroner. Norm joined Bing and the other detectives on the sidelines. The mood was sombre, everyone was quiet.

He starred at Bing. His watery eyes revealed his anguish. The flushed face and tight chin showed his anger. The demeanour of the other cops was similar.

Norm heard a thumping sound. He turned toward the road to locate the source of the noise. Inside the police tape was a cruiser with a young couple in the back seat. It was the baby's parents, Jolene and Kenny.

The father screamed and banged on the window with clenched fists. The mother was silent and zoned-out. She stared in the direction of the gruesome scene at the river's edge.

Norm wandered closer to the cruiser, where a female cop stood watch. He lifted his chin in a nod to acknowledge the officer, his gaze fixed on the young couple in the car. He thought Kenny might break the window with the bulky silver ring he wore on his right hand. To get a better look at Jolene, he walked around the car.

She was silent with her head down. Norm's shadow caused her to look up. Her eyes were almost swollen shut, her cheeks red and soaked with tears and snot. Strings of her hair were stuck to her face.

Not having children, he couldn't begin to imagine her pain. He eyeballed and considered Brewer again. Was he in pain? He displayed anger. Was it because Shay was dead or because he was one step closer to being labelled a baby killer?

Fourteen

Building a Case

Staff Sergeant Clarke called everyone at the scene together. The grizzled and seasoned detective appeared as though he'd lost his own child. His raspy voice was an octave lower than normal. He surveyed each cop in the group. The consternation in his eyes ripped holes in every one of them. He palmed his face with an open hand, as if moulding clay, and spewed his commands like an Army General before battle.

"Black and Simms, interviews, separate the parents and put them in different rooms. Go back to day one, get them to tell you everything they've done every minute of every hour of every day, until now. And do it by the book, this is a murder investigation now. Strom and Bingham—seize the car. Take the search warrant to the JP, or a Judge if the JP's not available."

Norm and Bing broke from the group. Clarke told two other detectives to prepare a search warrant for the parent's home. Bing already had the keys to a CIB car, so Norm jumped in with him. Rigid frame, clenched jaw and steely eyes, Bingham wasn't the same man Norm had worked with the day before. With two children, Norm could only imagine how Bingham felt.

With a death grip on the steering wheel, Bing stared straight ahead. They were almost at HQ when he broke the silence.

"Why can't we just go to TJ's and tow the fucking car? Its evidence of a crime and the pacifier's in plain view."

"By the book is what Wild Bill said. I've lost cases on bullshit technicalities, so I understand. The plain view doctrine might apply if the car was on the road, but it's on private property, and we were trespassing. Any evidence we find in the car would be inadmissible in court—fruit of the poison tree and all that crap."

Bing slowed down but blew through a red light without stopping.

"Poison tree? Who comes up with that shit?"

Norm checked his seat belt.

"Lawyers, we live in their world and they make the rules. If we get his prints or Shay's DNA on that pacifier Brewer's fucked. If he did this you don't want to give him a legal loophole, do you?"

His lips purple from compression, Bing shook his head. "I hear ya. Did you see that scumbag? He has baby-killer written all over him. I'd like to be in that interview room. He'd squeal like a pig."

Norm scoffed.

"That's why the boss won't let you anywhere near him. He's only been a person of interest until now, and other than being the last person to see the baby, we don't have any evidence to call him a suspect, let alone a killer."

"Are you..."

"Don't get me wrong. There's no doubt in my mind that the little fucker did it, but we must build a case to prove it. That takes time and patience, grasshopper."

Back in the CIB office at HQ Norm perused the warrant and handed it to Bing.

"Give this a once over, then take it to the JP. You need to learn the routine. I've gotta make a call. One of my informants has been paging me."

While Bing read the warrant, Norm called Roger Storey. He answered on the first ring.

"You looking for me? Saw the unknown number on my caller ID."

"Must be nice, we don't even have that here at the cop shop. Lack of tax dollars because of scammers like you milking the system."

"Hey, I resemble that remark. What's up, copper?"

"I was hoping to talk to Jeffrey. I wanted to ask him about TJ's loaner car and if Brewer might have used it. Doesn't really matter now, we're getting a warrant to seize it. Found the missing baby in the river this morning."

"So that's what all the commotion's about. I saw a bunch of cop cars and news trucks when I went to the corner store this morning. You think Brewer did it?"

"Officially, I can't say, but if you're asking me..."

"Never mind. Jeffrey says he did it."

Norm paused for a second, slid a pad of paper in front of him and grabbed his pen.

"Why's he say that?"

"I dunno...attitude, I guess. Jeffrey said TJ asked the boys if one of them used the loaner car, but no one admitted to it. Said a customer wanted it, but complained it smelled like someone puked in it. Brewer's been hanging out at the shop. He said he had to get away from all the cops and media cuz they're stressing him out. Jeffrey says he didn't seem too broken up about the baby, complained about the lack of action from his old lady."

Norm stared into the empty space between the top of the office desks and tiled ceiling and digested what had been said.

"Anything else? Do they have to ask for the loaner car?"

"They're supposed to, but Jeffrey snuck it out before, and he knows Brewer has too and bragged about banging some chick in it when Jolene was on the rag."

"Nice. No wonder the car stinks."

The Deputy Chief walked into the office and made a beeline toward Norm.

"Thanks, Roger, one of the big dogs is coming my way. I gotta go."

The Deputy stopped at the S/Sgt's desk, beside Norm's.

"Have you seen Clarke?"

"Yes, sir. At the crime scene with the Coroner. He addressed the troops and gave us all assignments. He's probably still out there. Do you want me to have him call you?"

The second in command looked around the room, as if he was searching for the answer.

"Yes. Tell him the media's driving me crazy. He needs to release a statement ASAP."

"Will do, sir. If I can't get him on the radio, I'll tell him personally, we're on the way..."

He'd already turned to walk away, waved a hand through the air in response. Norm was about to go looking for Bing when he appeared with the warrant in hand.

"We're good to go, Storm."

He picked up the car keys and radio from the desk, and they headed out.

Both bay doors were wide open at TJ's body shop, the shrill whine of a power tool pierced the still morning air. The weatherman had promised it wouldn't be as soupy as the previous day.

The loaner car was parked in the same spot, Bing pulled into the lot and stopped behind it. Norm saw the cruiser that'd been watching it, parked across and down the street. He held up a hand, signalling the officer to stay put for the time being.

Like an anxious dog on a leash, Bing charged at the car. TJ was in the garage, unaware of the police presence because of the noise around him. He was bent over a car fender, working it with a grinder. His ponytail hung out the back of the dew rag that was wrapped around his head. Colourful tattoos covered his arms like wallpaper.

An employee caught his eye with a wave and pointed to the cops. TJ shut off the power tool, straightened and stretched his back. He flipped the safety goggles to the top of his head and walked out to meet the interlopers.

Before he could speak, Bing waved the piece of paper for him to see.

"We have a search warrant. We're taking the Chevy."

TJ moved closer, paused to wipe dust or sweat from his eyes with the back of his hand. Norm stepped between the two men, fearing a clash of tempers.

"Before you get all wound up, sir, let me explain. We know that Kenneth Brewer works for you, and we have reason to believe that he used your loaner car in the commission of a crime."

The shop owner froze in thought, considered the statement, and was about to answer when Norm continued.

"We saw a pacifier in the back seat, and this morning we found a dead baby in the river."

TJ's face muscles relaxed, and his lower jaw dropped, parting his lips. He narrowed his eyes and gawked at the car.

"Was it Brewer's kid?"

Bing was already inside the car.

Norm answered. "We're not at liberty to speculate at this time, your guess is as good as mine. We'd like to talk to you and your employees about this car. I understand they have access to it."

He continued to stare at the car in silence, he avoided eye contact with Norm. TJ was not the same man they'd met the previous night. Breaking the trance, he craned his neck to see what Bing put into an evidence bag. It was the pacifier.

TJ turned to Norm, his eyes searching the ground at his feet.

"Whatever you need, officer. Brewer's not here. I never really liked that kid. I let him and Jeffrey use the car when it wasn't loaned out, but they're supposed to ask me first."

Fifteen

Paperwork

After having the car towed from TJ's, Norm and Bing headed back to the barn for another briefing. Clarke called everyone in for an update at 1300 hours. Famished, and with only twenty minutes to spare, the two Detectives slipped through the Tim Horton's drive through and grabbed a couple of sandwiches to go. Not knowing what task awaited them at the office, they ate in the car, on the way.

The only sound came from paper wrappers and chewing. Norm saw that Bing was still upset. Obviously, he was thinking about his own children and wondering how any father, or any person at all, could kill a baby. Before getting married, Norm and his wife had agreed that neither of them was interested in having children. They spent their money on travel and home renovations.

He imagined one of his siblings being murdered, but somehow it wasn't the same, he couldn't comprehend a parent's pain. His middle sister had gone missing when she was a child. Norm had been responsible for keeping an eye on her. She returned after a few hours with the tale of a stranger offering her candy for a ride. His identity and any further details were never known.

Strom had no personal comparison for the case at hand. It was no wonder the other cops who had children were so angry. He thought about the old days, before cameras and constitutional rights, and the beating a suspected baby killer would have received.

It was expected back then, by cops and bad guys alike. The world had changed, murderers were set free on technicalities or insanity pleas. It was utter madness that drove many cops to drink.

More absurdity lay ahead, the news media had police headquarters surrounded. They resembled an Apache war party using microphones for arrows, aimed at Staff Sergeant Clarke on the front steps of the building. Bing ran the gauntlet of news vehicles that were parked along both sides of the street and stashed the unmarked car in a spot marked for police vehicles only.

To avoid the media storm out front, they snuck in the back door. Norm's wife and one of her co-workers came out the same door, on their way to lunch. He paused to chat for a minute.

Bing held the door, alternating his gaze between his watch and his partner. Norm got the hint and followed him into the building. He and Sandra never really discussed work at home. She knew the score.

The Criminal Investigation Branch seemed more like a church. Detectives who usually towered over file cabinets and desks, were hunched over and spoke in hushed voices. Some typed, while others wrote in their notebooks. Bing went directly to his desk, Norm pulled up a chair beside it. They had their own reports to complete.

Staff Sergeant Clarke walked in five minutes past the hour. He'd aged five years since Norm had seen him earlier at the crime scene. The man who everyone respected and feared, sat down at his desk and buried his face in his hands. He massaged his forehead with his fingertips and puffed air from between his palms. Wild Bill gazed around the room, took stock of the stern faces, and searched for words.

"Listen up, people. Forget about the vultures outside, the phone calls, and questions from your co-workers or loved ones. We've got a dead baby in the morgue and the asshole who did it in our interview room. You know what we gotta do. It's a circumstantial case at best, but we've got enough pieces of the puzzle to solve it."

He glared at Detective's Black and Simms.

"Do I need to tell you how a confession would make my day?"

Black answered. "No, sir. We were gonna question the mother first, she hasn't stopped balling since we brought her in. Brewer appears to be sleeping in the other room."

Clarke nodded.

"You know what that tells you; that guilty little shit. Try Ms. Lockwood again. I want a proper statement from her now that we found the baby. Use her against him. Make shit up if you have to."

He scanned the room again.

"By the way folks, there's no doubt on the ID. The deceased had webbed toes on one foot and they were able to get a print from the other. It's baby Shay. Coroner says there's signs of trauma; shit that happened before she went in the water."

Heads with short haircuts shook in dismay and someone mumbled, "fucking asshole."

Norm saw Bing's eyes water.

Clarke barked. "Okay, gentlemen, get to work."

Black and Simms picked up their files and headed for the interview rooms. The Investigations Inspector sauntered over to Clarke's desk and they had a private conversation. Norm and Bing worked on their evidentiary and supplementary reports.

With his paperwork complete, and stomach growling again, Norm surveyed the office. He was alone. Bing had mumbled something to him and wandered off. He got up from his chair, stretched and rubbed his lower back with the heels of his palms. The clock said it was near quitting time, almost dinner time. He knew better than to leave without asking Wild Bill first.

He twisted his neck from side to side to get the kinks out, then aimed for the elevator. The lunch room was empty too, most of the civilian staff had gone home for the day. Norm fumbled around in his pocket and found enough coin for a pop and chocolate bar. A sugar fix to keep him going.

Taking the stairs back down, he swung by the interview rooms and literally bumped into his boss, Hayes, in the hallway.

"Hey, Norm, were your ears ringing?"

He had a mouth full of Snickers.

"Huh?"

"I was just talking to S/Sgt. Clarke, asked him if you're ever coming back to Drugs. You still work for me, don't you?"

Norm swallowed a gulp of Pepsi to wash down the chocolate bar.

"I don't know, what'd Wild Bill say?"

Hayes patted Norm on the shoulder, then started to walk away.

He looked back and guffawed.

"Ask him."

He offered a half-assed salute and carried on. Norm poked the last hunk of chocolate into his mouth. He peered through the window into the interview room where Jolene Lockwood was sitting with a policewoman.

The young mother stared silently into space. Hers hands clung to a wad of soggy tissue. Her cheeks were red and puffy, eyes only thin slits. She moved back and forth in her chair, as if she was rocking her baby to sleep.

Norm entered the viewing area, between the two interview rooms. Wild Bill gawked at Kenneth Brewer behind the one-way glass. He was in with Black and Simms. The man's demeanour was nothing like his girlfriend's. Rigid in his chair, arms folded across his chest, he stared at the table that was between him and the Detectives. It wasn't a look of angst or anger on his face. He appeared bored.

"What's going on? They getting anything from him?"

Clarke's intense gaze remained on Brewer.

"Over two hours and they've got nothing. Says he's got nothing to hide. Does he look like a guy who's got nothing to hide? Says he may have taken a bag of garbage out that night, but was too drunk to remember. Won't admit to using TJ's car the same night. Once, on another occasion, but not that night. Remembers that in his drunken stupor."

Norm surveyed the room. Each Detective has their own routine and are particular about how they set up an interview room. Black and Simms had Brewer backed into the far corner. He was a few feet away from the table. The two detectives sat on the opposite side.

Black was attired in a charcoal grey suit with fine pinstripes. It appeared to have just come off the store rack. His face and neck were red. His tie was either too tight or his frustration and anger were showing.

Simms paid attention to his notebook. He looked more relaxed, with his shirtsleeves rolled up and tie loosened. It was almost as if he was bored, tired, and ready to go home.

Wild Bill shook his head, rubbed the side of his face with one hand.

"Your boss says you're pretty good at this."

Norm turned to Clarke.

"Interviews?"

"Says you have a way with lowlife. They respond to you and that's why you have more informants than anyone else on the job."

"Maybe. I've had some luck. I treat them like I'd want to be treated, with respect. That's all they really want."

Wild Bill turned and put a hand on Norm's shoulder.

"I'm gonna tell my guys to take a break, but I'll leave the tape running. We're gonna go for coffee. What you do with your time while we're gone is up to you."

He offered a flat grin, nodded, and tapped on the glass. Black and Simms packed up their files and met Clarke at the door.

Sixteen

Show & Tell

The three men left for coffee. Norm stayed put and continued to watch for a few minutes. When the Detectives left the room, Brewer closed his eyes and dropped his chin to his chest, as if he was about to take a nap.

Norm slinked into the room. He took Black's chair and swung it around to one side of the table, putting himself close to Brewer, with no obstructions between them.

The suspect pretended he was sleeping at first, but his eyes popped open with the invasion of his personal space. It was an intentional move by Norm, he wanted to be noticed. He didn't say a word, wore a poker face, and casually eyed the man. Brewer checked out his new guest from head to toe. He paused and grinned when he saw the shoes.

It was Norm's queue.

"Great sneakers, eh?"

Brewer was wearing the same brand of footwear. His pose relaxed, arms dropped, and he folded his hands in his lap.

He continued. "Make you feel like you're walking on marshmallows. Thin guy like you can probably outrun a fat guy like me."

The grin became a smirk. Norm had his attention.

Brewer's eyes showed he was puzzled by the cop's attire.

"They let Detectives dress like that now?" Referring to Norm's tee shirt, jeans, and running shoes.

"No, I'm not a Dick like the guys who just left, I'm a Narc."

He tried to throw Brewer off his game and make him feel like he was the most important guy in the room. Demean himself and the other cops if necessary, to build rapport.

"A Narc. What are you doing in here?"

"The Dicks are shorthanded so they asked me to sit with you while they went to fix their hair and polish their shoes."

Brewer chuckled.

Norm didn't let up.

"Guess they figured if I'm in here with you, I'm not out busting grade-schoolers for smoking pot on their lunch hour."

With Brewer relaxed and paying attention, he changed tactics.

"Hey man, I'm really sorry to hear about your daughter...Shay was her name?"

His eyes rounded and his head dropped an inch. He didn't answer the question.

"I can't imagine your pain, losing a child like that. How's your wife doing? I saw her next door talking to some other Dicks."

Brewer tilted his head, pondered the question like it was the first time he'd thought about what Jolene might say about everything.

"She's not my wife...we moved in together when she had the baby. Can I talk to her?"

"Not my call, man. I can ask the Dicks when they get back. She looked pretty upset...finding out what happened to her baby girl. You must be upset too."

He feigned a look of concern.

"You would be too if you lost a kid."

Norm noted how Brewer distanced himself, never referring to his daughter by her name.

"Like I said, I can't imagine your pain, having no children myself."

He changed direction again.

"TJ says you're pretty good with auto body work. You like it there?"

"He can be an asshole, but I like the job. Keeps my mind off other things. I'm working on my own car."

"The '72 Mustang?"

Brewer leaned in, slid his hands down his thighs. His eyes smiled.

"Yeah, the motor's in good shape, but if you saw the body, it's brutal. TJ lets me work on it when things are slow in the shop. He's good like that."

"The first car I bought when I got on the job was a '77 Grand Prix. The last year of the big ones; 350, 4-barrel."

"Sweet. Still got it?"

"No. Moved on...needed a truck. Hey, do you get to drive some of the cool cars that come into the shop?"

Brewer rolled his eyes.

"No... maybe, when the boss ain't around."

"I hear you get to use the loaner car too, when the boss ain't around. Jeff said you guys use it as a shagging wagon."

He blinked and broke eye contact, searched his memory for the appropriate answer and wondering what Jeff might have said.

"Yeah, but that was a long time ago, before I moved in with Jolene."

"C'mon, don't bullshit a bull shitter. He said you weren't getting any at home so you banged some skank in the car and she left a snail trail on the seat. Hey, it's okay in my book. You're not married, and you got your needs, right?"

Norm could almost hear the wheels turning in Brewer's head. He hit him harder.

"Hey, did the Dicks tell you they found a baby pacifier in the loaner car. They're testing it for DNA. Pretty amazing what they can do with that shit these days."

Brewer remained silent. He clutched his hands in his lap, rubbed his thumbs together.

"You know they're going to find out it belonged to Shay, don't you? And they told you they have a witness who saw you leaving your house with a garbage bag. And they seized your old running shoes about an hour ago. Looks like they match the prints in the mud by the river, you know, where they found Shay."

It was a lie. Norm threw in the last part for good measure. He noticed that Brewer's head was moving. He nodded subconsciously; agreeing with what was being said. It was exactly what Norm was waiting for. He slid his chair closer to the suspect and leaned into him. He spoke softly.

"I told you I don't have kids, but I know what it's like. I raised my five younger siblings."

Brewer avoided eye contact and rocked slightly in his chair.

"I know what it's like when they're babies...crying all the time. You can't sleep. I remember putting my pillow over my head, trying to drown out the noise...counting the seconds between screams, waiting to see if it would ever stop."

Brewer continued nodding, it was more pronounced. His hands on his thighs, his fingers dug in and turned white at the knuckles. Out of the corner of one eye, Norm saw a shadow at the bottom of the door. He heard the sound of dragging chairs on the other side of the wall. They were back.

"Kenny, I feel your pain. You're not even sure if the kid's yours and then it's in your house...in your face day and night. Shitty diapers, the constant screaming and crying...you can't even hear your television."

Brewer's breathing grew deep and heavy, his neck flushed red.

"My one little sister drove me crazy. I just wanted to shake her until she stopped...even thought about smothering her with a pillow. I just needed some sleep and to make it stop."

Brewer's face grew beet red, his eyes glazed.

"It must have driven you crazy, Kenny. Jolene out drinking with her mother, leaving the little brat with you. Why should you have to take care of her kid? All it did was eat, and shit, and scream, and cry. Is that what happened, Kenny?"

His right knee started to bounce uncontrollably, and his eyes bulged.

"Kenny, I feel your pain, man. Is that what happened? The little bitch wouldn't stop crying...drove you crazy...until..."

Brewer grabbed his head as if it was about to explode and burst into a rage.

"Yes! She was driving me nuts. I couldn't take it anymore. I was drinking and had almost passed out, but she was so fucking loud. The screaming hurt my head so I turned up the TV. I had to do something, I just wanted it to stop."

His nostrils flared and spittle flew freely from his lips as he shouted.

"I didn't know what to do...I grabbed her from the crib and yelled at her and shook her to make her stop. I..."

The words caught in his throat and it seemed like it was the first time he realized what he'd done. He sat back in his chair and took a deep breath. The red slowly dissipated from his face. Brewer put his head down.

He spoke softly.

"I'm sorry."

Seventeen

Guilty

The coroner's report said that baby Shay was shaken and beaten to death, then stuffed into a garbage bag and tossed into the Detroit River. Kenneth Brewer's defence counsel argued he was an immature man who suffered from psychiatric problems and alcohol abuse. The baby's death was accidental. He meant it no harm.

During the trial Jolene Lockwood testified as to her boyfriend's generally bad behaviour towards herself and her baby, Shay. She avoided eye contact with him during the court proceedings, but she was distraught and cried continuously. She had to be escorted from the courtroom on more than one occasion.

A jury of his peers took less than a day to convict Kenneth Brewer of manslaughter. He was sentenced to ten years in federal penitentiary.

Jolene Lockwood was forced to move back in with her mother until she got knocked up again and put herself back into the welfare system. She remained a single mother for years until she met a decent man who had two kids of his own.

After serving the recommended mandatory time behind bars Brewer applied for early parole. He was refused by the board and had to serve his full sentence. Like most baby killers and child molesters, he was not treated well by other inmates. If there is one thing that hardened criminals cannot stomach, it's a coward who harmed a defenceless child. Even the worst offenders have a code of honour.

Upon his release from prison Brewer relocated to a city somewhere between Windsor and Toronto, and he was never heard from again.

Eighteen

Karma

Twenty-two years after the hot and humid summer of baby Shay's disappearance, Norm Strom lounged poolside in Mexico, enjoying his retirement. While reading news from home on his laptop he saw an article about a man who was found dead in a known crack house in downtown Windsor. He was found severely beaten.

The deceased was identified as Kenneth Brewer.

"Designated Hitters"

One

Dangerous

The headline read, "Killer's Dangerous Offender Appeal Denied." The Windsor Star reported the Supreme Court of Canada shot down a bid by convicted killer Donald Gates, whom a judge once described as an incurable psychopath, to have his dangerous offender status overturned.

The decision by the country's highest court meant the two-time murdering scum would remain in jail for the rest of his natural life. Nodding to himself, Norm Strom thought maybe the judicial system did work on the rare occasion. The newspaper article was short, and he skimmed through it.

The waitress placed his breakfast in front of him. He salivated at the pungent aroma of fried bacon on his plate. Getting a piece of the pork fat into his cakehole was more important than the fate of Donny Gates. He folded and stuffed a slice of heaven into his mouth. The retired Detective arranged his plate the way he liked it; bacon, eggs and tomato slices each in their own section. It was a low carb day.

Breakfast was a just reward for a grueling workout at the gym. His forehead still warm and damp with sweat, Norm dabbed it with a napkin. He accepted his daily workouts as penance for the two previous months he'd spent exploring South America, indulging in Chilean and Argentinian food and wine.

Norm was into his third year of life after work, and he loved every minute of it. He'd been to Southeast Asia and did a motorcycle trip to Alaska the year before that. They said he'd get bored, so he'd tried part-time work with a wine tour company and drove a shuttle for a car dealership, but work got in the way of travel plans.

His mind drifted back to his days working Drouillard Road, the stomping grounds for guys like Donny Gates. It was a tough neighborhood and there was plenty of action for cops who liked to work.

He remembered patrolling with different partners. Buck was first, a veteran who showed him the ropes. His steady partner, Digger, came a year later. There were the rookies, with whom he shared his acquired knowledge of the street.

Faces flashed through his mind like a motion picture in fast-forward. Not only the men and women he worked with, but the hundreds of criminals that he'd busted and sent to jail. He remembered whole families of degenerates, and dirt bags like Donny Gates.

Two

Home Alone

Donald (Donny) Gates stared at the grey cement slab five feet in front of him. A stainless-steel toilet adorned the wall to his right. The glass door on his left offered his only view—the cell identical to his directly across the hall. The baron cubicle was home for the rest of his natural life.

He sat expressionless. There was no hint of any frustration or disappointment in the news he'd exhausted his last appeal. Eyes resembling Charles Manson's challenged the wall and like high-powered lasers tried to burn a hole through it. The muffled echoes of steel doors and men's voices rang hollow in his ears. It was as close as Gates would ever come to the sound of silence.

He transferred to Millhaven Correctional Institute from the defunct Kingston Penitentiary. The two institutions were different beasts but born of the skin and bones of the same ancestors. Both were maximum security to house society's worst criminals and, as in Gate's case, dangerous offenders.

He'd played all his cards and was out of the game for good. No more court appeals, no chance at ever being free again. He wasn't surprised by his fate. He knew he deserved to be exactly where he was. *Fuck the world,* he thought, *I had a good run.*

Donny spent years in similar rooms to this one. Being wild at heart, he hated the routine that came with incarceration. He didn't have any friends or family to miss, some were also in jail, others dead.

Being labelled a Dangerous Offender meant he had no chance of parole. He wondered how long he would live and what 'life in prison' would really mean for him. Gates never showed remorse for any of his crimes—not even the murders. He had no regrets. 'Shit happens' was his motto.

If he did it all over again, would he tackle life the same way? Probably. His destiny was to fail. It wasn't just him, his sister was a drug abusing slut, and his two half-brothers were habitual criminals serving time in other penal institutions. His dad had long passed, but mom carried on the family tradition of selling booze or drugs and fencing stolen property.

Donny Gates was born fucked for life. It didn't bother him. He thrived on being feared and revered on the street. He enjoyed doing whomever and whatever he wanted. It was life in the D, a hard-core neighborhood that was Ford City before annexation. A lunch-bucket town with Drouillard Road as its backbone.

He thought hard about who he might miss while tucked away for eternity. His family was as screwed up as him; they reaped what they sewed. The only real friend to speak of was Brian Lalonde. Donny couldn't remember that last time he'd seen him. He thought it was years earlier when they served time in the same jail.

Maybe he should have been more like Brian—a natural athlete who could have played professional hockey or baseball. Too bad the dumbass was a follower and went along with every stupid idea Gates hatched. Donny took no responsibility for Brian's failures. The man made his own choices.

He remembered meeting Brian when they played baseball on the same Little League team. Gates made the roster because they were short on players. He could play the game but had no desire to excel at it. He hated the uniform and the fact there were so many stupid rules.

Lalonde was different, he was a team player and the best hitter in the league. He played shortstop, and when he wasn't batting cleanup, he was the designated hitter.

Brian unwittingly helped Donny earn his only suspension. For no reason, Gates disliked a guy on an opposing team. He told Brian they had to get the asshole before the game was over. After the guy hit a single that put him on first base, Donny told Brian to aim for the runner's head when he made the throw to second.

Another single forced the runner to second base. Brian fielded the ground ball and made a hard throw at the runner's head, like his friend had asked. The kid ducked when he slid into the base and Donny made the catch higher than he'd hoped.

He punched the guy in the face and broke his nose claiming it was an accident; his glove connected when he tried to make the tag. The umpire saw it for what it was, and Gates was ejected from the game.

He laughed when he saw blood gushing down the kid's face and the front of his jersey. When the official threatened a longer suspension, Donny peeled off his team shirt and threw it at him. That was the last baseball game he ever played.

Lalonde played for a few more years, becoming an all-star and one of the best ball players in the city. Although athletic, Brian wasn't the wisest owl in the barn. His lack of interest in school allowed him more time to hang out with his pal Donny.

Since neither came from affluent families, shoplifting and petty thievery became their favorite pastime. Like Donny, Brian also lacked moral support at home. His father was a truck driver who spent long hours on the road, and his mother was a drunk.

Gates' institutionalized internal clock told him the lights would go out any minute. He laid back on his cot and stared at a cement ceiling as grim as the walls. With nothing else to see, Donny closed his eyes to a darker shade of grey.

Three

Batter Up

Too many years had passed to recall the minute details, but Norm never forgot the first time he'd heard of Donny Gates and Brian Lalonde. It was the end of March 1994, his seventh year on the blue team. Windsor Police covered the city from two locations: Downtown (Station #1 or Headquarters) and the Precinct (Station #2). Walker Road was the line that separated the two halves. He was assigned to Headquarters.

For an action junkie, the 7pm to 3am shift was a dream come true. On that watch, working overtime was common with tours running up to twelve hours instead of the scheduled eight. Called the Delta shift, it overlapped afternoons and midnights, keeping cops on the street during the changeover.

Friday night guaranteed a steady stream of calls for service. Norm worked with a veteran who also hated midnights, and like Norm, he traded for the overlap tour. On that night he and Norm were the only car covering the whole west side of the city during shift change. If backup was needed, they'd have to wait for a car to be dispatched from the lineup room downtown.

A half hour after booking into service they received their first call, a burglar alarm at a downtown business. They found it secure, a false alarm. The next two calls came back to back, disorderlies, typical for a Friday night.

Two and a half hours into their shift, they were called in for lunch. On busy nights they often went without relief and to avoid hunger, their meal was squeezed in between calls or while writing reports.

When Norm and his partner booked back into service, they were sent to handle a Break & Enter. While completing the paperwork for that call they were dispatched to another B & E in progress. There was no backup available, all the other car crews were changing shifts. The perpetrator was gone by the time they arrived, disappearing with some jewelry and twelve bottles of beer.

By one-thirty in the morning, they'd handled another alarm and a fight call. One of the combatants in that altercation was arrested for causing a disturbance and transported to the police station. After completing their arrest report, they handled two more calls, a domestic, and a fight call on the east side of the city.

The Precinct was shorthanded that night, so the dispatcher used them to fill the void. Their next call was for an injured person on Drouillard Road, they were sent to backup Precinct units already on the scene.

On arrival Norm recognized the building. It was the clubhouse of the Knights motorcycle gang. The Precinct Patrol Sergeant said the chapter's president chased two neighborhood punks down the street to a vacant lot, where they cornered and beat him to death with baseball bats. Norm and his partner were assigned to cover the front and back doors of the club, ensuring that no one entered or left the scene.

Norm knew about the clubhouse and some of its members, it was required learning for an astute street cop. The Knights weren't the worst bad guys and easily the least violent of the three motorcycle gangs operating in the city at the time.

Prior to becoming a cop, he met a couple members through friends and acquaintances. For the most part, the club consisted of a group of motorcycle enthusiasts who liked to party. Some had criminal records, but most held regular jobs.

Norm stood posted inside the front door, a solid slab of steel with only a peephole. Visitors rang a buzzer for entry. He scanned the solemn faces inside the clubhouse and recognized three men. Two worked at the Drop-In Tavern. While off-duty, Norm put in a few hours there to pick up extra cash. The third was the son of a Windsor Police Sergeant. They grew up in the same neighborhood, and he met the guy's father on the job. Norm did his best to avoid eye contact.

There were about twenty people in the club. Most had entered after hours when other bars closed for the night. Visitors were only allowed entry and served alcohol if one of the Knights vouched for them. Police knew of the club's bootlegging activities but couldn't get past the locked door to enforce liquor laws.

It was unusually quiet for a barroom, those who talked amongst themselves did so in hushed voices. It was a cross between a recreation room in a private home and a small pub. A glass beer cooler lit up the area behind the custom-made wooden bar. A video monitor displayed the live feed from the camera mounted outside the front door.

Across the room, neon lights glowed on a muted jukebox. Booths lined the same wall, and those seated in them shared only whispers. They'd been told they weren't allowed to leave the premises, and knew the cops were serious, after witnessing two of the distraught and irate bikers dragged off in handcuffs.

Standing there, Norm remembered a time before he was cop when he drove a friend to a blind pig just around the corner. There was always somewhere to get a drink around Drouillard Road. It had been that way for decades. The home that Norm visited used its living room as a barroom. Men from the nearby Ford plant frequented the bootlegger on their lunch hours and breaks.

The decor was nothing fancy in the Knights clubhouse. Behind the bar Confederate and skull and crossbones flags bracketed the gang's coat of arms on the wall.

A Detective appeared from the curtained area at the back of the room. That was the shag-shack or bunk room for the bikers and their bitches. The veteran Dick escorted a woman back to her seat, then approached Norm.

Detective Smith wanted witnesses taken downtown for proper statements. He called in the cop who was posted outside the front door and told Norm to fetch his partner and take two of the witnesses to H.Q. Norm considered taking the cop's son and eyeballed him. The guy cringed and ducked as if trying to crawl under the table.

Norm and his partner asked the two men from the Drop-In to accompany them downtown. Heads hung low, they didn't say a word and went along. Norm tried to make small talk in the car, but only received shrugs and headshakes in response. When he asked if they knew who got beat up, one mumbled the name Tommy Valiant, the club's president. They offered nothing more, both stared out their windows.

The witnesses were separated at Headquarters and put into individual interview rooms. As Norm was about to leave the one who had spoken up earlier blurted out what Norm recognized as a baseball term.

The man said, "It was the designated hitters."

The witness lifted his head and offered a cold stare that settled somewhere beyond Norm. He moistened his lips and clarified, saying that two neighborhood tough guys did it. That's what he'd heard.

The next night at roll call, the Sergeant updated the outgoing shift on the status of the previous night's killing on Drouillard Road. He said that Brian Lalonde had been arrested by Homicide Detectives, and that his accomplice, Donny Gates, was wanted for that murder.

Four

Ford City

Years after the murder, Norm Strom was assigned to district seven. It was part of Station #2. The western boundary was the railway tracks that ran parallel to Walker Road. The CN tracks, south of Wyandotte Street, formed the north, east was Pillette Road, and Tecumseh Road was the south boundary. The patrol area included the housing projects on Central Avenue and the mixed residential/commercial area surrounding Drouillard Road.

It was densely populated with lower to middle income families in neighborhoods that were separated by automotive factories and their feeder plants. The heart of the district was where Walkerville and Ford City neighborhoods meshed together and formed part of East Windsor.

In its heyday Drouillard Road supported a dozen bars, watering holes that quenched the thirst of autoworkers from Ford, General Motors and Chrysler. The bars and the bootleggers in the area dispensed more booze than all the Essex and Kent licensed establishments combined.

Blue-collar workers blowing off steam with an abundance of readily-available alcohol, resulted in many boil-overs. That's where the cops came in, to clean up the mess. For the most part Drouillard Road took care of its own. The cops were called as a last resort, when things got completely out of hand.

There wasn't much along the road to see. Many commercial buildings sat vacant or had been boarded up. One small diner served those who wanted to eat something other than bar food. The bakery sold wholesale to grocery stores; its front window barred after years of break-ins. The linen supply business next door wore a similar iron girdle, as did the hardware store down the street.

The D smelled as gritty as it looked, especially on days where there was no breeze to carry away the foul emissions that spewed from the Ford foundry's smokestacks. Fine soot permeated the air and coated parked cars and buildings for blocks around. Company employees received vouchers to have their cars detailed, to clean and preserve their paint.

Norm was assigned to seven district a few years after the murder at the Knights clubhouse. Gates and Lalonde were safely tucked away in jail, serving seven-year sentences for manslaughter. That's what the mild-mannered biker's life was deemed to be worth, seven years. If paroled early, they would only serve two-thirds of that.

Strom learned the ropes in the hard-core hood from veteran Buck (Joe) Flynn. His regular partner was on indefinite leave so Norm volunteered to fill the void. A grunt from Buck acknowledged that he was okay with the partnership. He was old school, a tough street cop who was handed a revolver, Billy club, and handcuffs and told to go get em.

In Buck's heyday more justice was doled out on the streets than in the courts. That's the way it was. Criminals expected and respected that it was the law of the land. There was less petty crime and offenders knew they'd pay a price when caught. There was no probation or house arrest back then.

Assessing Buck's various moods and facial expressions on any given day was like watching a live stage production. Hard as steel on the outside, he was soft as marshmallow on the inside. He had one mug that scared Norm. A *Dirty Harry* scowl. He raised one eyebrow and no words were necessary.

After years of layoffs and factory closings, the number of bars on Drouillard dwindled to six; an impressive number for a strip less than half a kilometer long. It wasn't just dirt bags who lived in the area, there were many hard-working families who'd resided there for generations. Buck knew the good, the bad, and the ugly in the D.

On a sunny Sunday afternoon Buck drove into an alley near Richmond and St. Luke. Norm noticed smoke pouring out of an aluminum shed and thought his partner was taking him to the scene of a fire. Buck introduced Norm to Nick, the neighborhood barbecue king.

If you wanted a lamb, pig, or even a turkey done on a spit, he was the guy to see. His backyard storage unit had been converted into a giant rotisserie where he could cook six large carcasses at a time.

Nick was a loveable Hungarian who drank as much as he cooked. He always offered a beer and a shot whenever Buck and Norm stopped by to see what was on the spit. Their excuse to abstain was that they were on duty. That worked most of the time. Nick sold some of the meat at one of the local taverns.

Buck ordered a whole pig from Nick for a summer shift party he threw at his place in Amherstburg. Norm was so impressed that he went to Nick for his own oinker, and for a big turkey at Christmas. It was the best bird ever. Whenever the two cops drove by his house and smelled something cooking, it was difficult not to stop. Samples were always graciously given.

Norm had over eight years' experience under his belt, but still learned from Buck. He had an uncanny ability to sniff out bad guys who were up to no good. Patrolling around the bars in their district was one way to find trouble. Norm learned people entering a tavern weren't usually a problem, it was the ones who came out. The ones who'd consumed copious amounts of alcohol.

Police could stop someone on a hunch or a gut feeling in those days. It was a no-brainer when someone exited a bar and climbed behind the wheel of a motor vehicle. On one occasion

Buck pointed to two guys in an old beat-up car, in the alley behind one of the bars.

He gave Norm the look and said, "They're up to no good."

The driver refused to stop when Norm activated the roof lights, and the chase was on. It was the wildest vehicle pursuit Norm had ever experienced. The suspects blew through stop signs and traffic lights and rolled over lawns. They drove on the wrong side of a divided road, crashed through construction barricades, and bounced off other cars stopped in heavy traffic.

The fleeing vehicle nearly ran over a police officer who'd set up a roadblock. He was standing outside his cruiser with his gun pointed at the automobile bearing down on him. Buck fired a few rounds at the fleeing car trying to stop it, but the chase continued into rush hour traffic. At the time police were under scrutiny for high speed pursuits and discharging their firearms at and from moving vehicles.

Buck's gut instinct panned out. When finally stopped, the fleeing driver had no documentation for the car he drove and was an escaped convict from a correctional facility in British Columbia. They'd been drinking in the car and had a replica pistol in the glove box.

The police administration accepted Buck's reasons for the chase, but shortly after the incident new government legislation banned cops from shooting at motor vehicles. Years later, police received even stricter guidelines from the government to abolish high speed pursuits.

Five

Memory Lane

After breakfast Norm paid his bill and bought five bucks worth of Nevada tickets. He pealed back two and found three cherries. The winnings were reinvested, and he received more losers, but he walked away satisfied he'd donated to a worthy charity.

With a few errands to run, the retired Detective drove west along Tecumseh Road. He passed through his old stomping grounds in what had been Sandwich East, before it was annexed by Windsor.

The old Fleming House had changed its name to Charly's. There'd been a bar on that corner longer than he'd been alive. Norm remembered the stale beer smell that drifted outside thanks to exhaust fans. He was just a kid and found the odor offensive while he waited for his mother on the sidewalk next door at Steve's Handy Food Market. Eventually he acquired a taste for the golden nectar of the gods.

His reward for not wandering off and into traffic was a raw hot dog plucked right from the package on the way home. To Norm, it was better than a Popsicle. Mom told him he'd get worms, but he figured that was one of those old wives' tales or catchy phrases not found in any encyclopedia. That was before the Internet. They were likely proverbs passed down in small rural towns like McGregor, where his mother had grown up.

Pepe, mom's father, had more colorful quotes. Statements like 'blacker than Toby's ass'; something that apparently wasn't considered a racial slur back in the day. He called some people 'dirty pot-lickers.' Norm never figured that one out.

His own father, who everyone affectionately called Weiner, added a touch of vulgarity when he was agitated and wanted to make a point. Two of his favorites were, 'suck me off with a breast pump' and 'stick it in your ass.'

As Norm passed the Giant Tiger, he tried to recall how many stores had previously occupied the site. There was Loblaw's, OK Economy, and a bulk/box store. Then it became a Shoprite catalog store. That was where he got his first job as a stock boy.

It was a great neighborhood to grow up in, the parking lot behind the store was perfect for playing strikeout and road hockey. He remembered one of the neighbors pinning bedsheets on the giant billboard at the back of the lot to show cartoons and movies. When heavy rain flooded the lot, kids created their own water sports.

There was a grass field behind the parking lot, which he accidentally set on fire, twice. It later became a condominium complex. After his divorce Norm dated a woman who lived in one of the units. When she offered him a tour and stepped out onto her balcony, he was shocked.

The view overlooked his old back yard. His house looked about the same, maybe a little more weathered than he remembered. It was hard to believe six kids grew up in such a small place.

So many memories came back to him. Throwing packages of ketchup from the KFC onto the road for cars to run over. Watching fast cars race past the Hi-Ho. His alma mater, Herman High School, was only a few blocks away.

Norm was always athletic and shined as a water polo star, making the all-city team, and then the provincial all-star team. They trained as the junior Olympic team. It seemed like a hundred years and almost as many pounds ago.

He drove past Central Avenue. The first house he bought was near Seminole Street. Purchased for thirty-six thousand dollars, when interest rates were at twenty-one and a half percent. Newly married at the time and having grown up on the east side, Norm didn't take the city housing projects down the street into consideration before buying. The complex changed the whole dynamic of the neighborhood.

With little coaxing, his car turned right onto Drouillard Road. The McDonald's on the corner was one of the first golden arches in Canada. Heading north on Drouillard from Tecumseh, was like driving up the tail of a dragon.

A seedy peeler bar having undergone several name changes, was a precursor for what lie ahead. At Seminole the mythical creature spreads its hind legs.

Crossing the railway tracks was like crawling up its butt and into the belly of the beast. The dragon's front claws were planted firmly in the turf between the junkyard and the railway viaduct at Wyandotte Street.

More grungy drinking establishments resembled the serpent's scaly epidermis. The Ford Foundry was the source of the fire that spewed from its mouth. Drouillard was nothing like the fairy-tale home of Puff the Magic Dragon.

Norm liked to think he had something to do with taming the man-eater in the seven years he worked the streets there. On his trip down memory lane, he recognized the skeletal remains of the D, but a lot had changed. The air lacked the old smell, since the foundry had been torn down.

Empty lots and buildings were artistically tended to like a collection of Easter eggs. Walls and courtyards resembled an open-air studio, where colorful sculptures and murals boasted the history of Ford City. The recording studio was still intact.

The recreation center buzzed with activity, but the old biker clubhouse sat empty. Only a couple a watering holes were still in operation. A thriving community garden filled a former vacant lot.

Norm chuckled to himself as he drove by the Sibley residence. How could he forget the night they and the Charbot's took their long-standing feud into the street? Cheryl Sibley was higher than a spy satellite and took to trashing a Charbot vehicle parked a few doors down from their house.

He and Digger Daniels were driving by at the time and stopped to arrest Cheryl. Mother Sibley and one of her boys played tug-of-war with the cops, trying to free their sister from their grasp and the arrest. The Sisley's fought the law, but the law won.

After the wrestling match mom accused Norm of stepping on and injuring her big toe. Upon leaving he tried to appease her by telling her not to worry, that they would call a tow truck.

Ah, the good old days. Norm thought about the murder near the clubhouse. He was always amazed that the bikers never sought retaliation for that. It didn't make sense, didn't any of them have the balls to avenge their president's death? Were they afraid of Gates and Lalonde or their families? The detectives thought the other bikers in jail would get to them, but it never happened.

Both men had siblings with lengthy criminal records, but none had the propensity for violence like the designated hitters—known enforcers in the hood.

Norm remembered Brian's brother, Jack. A common thief who stole from his own family and neighbors to support his drug and alcohol habits. Drunk or sober, he was gentle as a hamster and never gave the cops a hard time.

He couldn't say the same for Donny Gates.

Six

Brian's Song

Experts and convicts agree on the long-term effects of incarceration. It will either make you or break you. In Brian Lalonde's case it was the latter. Being a free spirit, he couldn't accept the confines of the bars and walls that caged him. While waiting in jail for his trial for manslaughter, his body began to fail him.

His only visitor was his lawyer. Brian's family was not the supportive type. It was no surprise that they didn't visit him. He thought his baseball coach might stay in touch, but neighborhood gossip and bad press kept him away. He'd already been convicted long before a jury of his peers could do it officially.

Baseball and hockey had kept his mind and body in good shape. The County Jail offered neither sport, only limited time to pace a small courtyard. The penitentiary was better with a large exercise yard and free weights.

Brian quickly learned there was a hierarchy among prisoners, and that he was at the bottom. He'd never made friends easily. Even his teammates didn't associate with him outside their games. Donny Gates was his only real buddy. He discovered that inmates don't make acquaintances, only enemies or alliances. There was no team concept.

Prison weathered Brian like the leaves on a hardwood tree in autumn. On the street he'd held his own and came out on top of every altercation he'd ever had. He lost his first fight in the pen, and with it, his respect. His lack of confidence and diminished body weight left him a target for jailhouse predators and bullies. Rumor had it that he submitted and became a prison bitch.

Brian Lalonde disappeared after his release. Everyone assumed he'd return to Drouillard Road and take his rightful place on the throne alongside Donny Gates, but he never returned to the kingdom. Upon his parole he was sent to a halfway house in London. A new course was charted for the retired designated hitter.

Some say he stayed on there to counsel other ex-cons and parolees. Others say that he became a long-distance truck driver, running loads across Canada. One rumor said that he'd contracted AIDS in prison and that he moved away to die in peace. Norm had heard various stories and figured the truth was probably a combination of them. In all honesty, he really didn't give a shit.

Seven

Three Strikes

He couldn't remember the exact dates, but Norm recalled arresting Donny Gates on at least three separate occasions after he was paroled. He only served five years of his seven-year sentence, apparently adequate punishment for viciously killing a man in Canada.

Donny didn't have to prove he had been rehabilitated. Since he hadn't killed anyone in prison and pinky-promised he'd behave if released, the parole board gave him their stamp of approval.

With no ambition or plan for the rest of his life, Gates returned to his beloved Drouillard Road. Norm had never met the man prior to his incarceration. He was surprised by his appearance, mistakenly assuming the characteristics and features of a typical monster.

Gates was small in stature and of average height yet intimidating to look at. Maybe it was his reputation. He had a wiry frame and his hair was cropped short. His brown eyes were so dark they resembled black holes. They were as empty as his soul.

Digger and Storm (their nicknames on the street) were the heavy hand of the law on Drouillard Road. They'd earned a reputation for their zero-tolerance attitude toward criminals and their bad behavior in the D. The cops worked together with a non-profit organization whose mission was to clean up the area and polish the neighborhood's tarnished name.

The boys in blue kept a recipe box in the cruiser's glove compartment. It was filled with index cards containing photos and information on the area's bad seeds. The dynamic duo carried their own Polaroid camera to snap photographs of persons of interest and add them to the file. They called it the 'magic box.' That was before computers or smartphones. The box was kept in the car around the clock so other officers assigned to the district could refer to it and add information to the files.

One afternoon Digger and Storm stopped Donny Gates and another known offender leaving Yesterday's Tavern. Knowing they were criminals was enough to stop and question them in those days. Norm adopted Dick's philosophy in dealing with criminals. Since they'd willingly made the decision to become what ailed society, it was naturally prudent to use any means available under the law to proactively protect the public from their scourge.

In other words, those with criminal records were first in line to make donations to provincial coffers in the form of tickets, warrants, and any other reasons for arrest. Having previous convictions for crime meant you were fair game to Daniels and Strom. They acknowledged that everyone made mistakes, and they gave hard-working citizens their share of breaks. Known offenders received no mercy.

Conditions of Donny Gates' parole included abstaining from alcohol and communicating with any known criminals. That afternoon in front of the tavern, Norm considered the fact that Gates knowingly drank alcohol and violated the first part of his release conditions. The second condition was almost comical since everyone Gates knew had a criminal record. He did not pass go and went directly back to jail.

"Correctional Institution" is a contradiction of terms. Hard-working taxpayers believe convicted criminals are punished by being incarcerated and that they are going to be rehabilitated while interned. There is some truth in the fact that criminals are penalized when put in jail, but no prisoner is ever corrected while inside.

Unfortunately, the same liberals who enact laws to incarcerate the dregs of society are the ones who believe the system can rehabilitate them, and that they should be given a chance at early release so that they might rejoin the same society they disrupted. It becomes a laughable paradox. The criminals receive a life sentence for murder, only to be paroled and released before the end of their time on earth.

People wonder why police officers become bitter. Norm remembered a guy his own age who'd grown up in his neighborhood. He'd lost track of him after becoming a cop but saw his name on the overnight arrest sheet one morning. The man had been arrested for killing his wife with a hammer. He was convicted of the crime and sentenced to life in prison, but only served seven years of his life sentence.

It was cheaper for him to kill her than to get a divorce. Financially, it cost him nothing to live in jail. Rent, food, and clothes were free. There was no division of property and no spousal support to pay.

When he got out of prison everything he had before he went in waited for him. He may have lost a few friends, but others welcomed him home and shared a good laugh at the expense of our justice system. Surely, his dead wife's family didn't see it that way.

Thinking he was making a difference by arresting Donny Gates for breaching his parole conditions and sending him back to jail, Norm was understandably pissed off when he saw him back on the street a short time later.

Nothing had changed. He was still drinking and hanging out with whomever he wanted. Norm was more than happy to arrest him again, thinking maybe they'd revoke his parole the second time, like they were supposed to do when someone ignored the board's release conditions.

Norm stopped for the red light on Drouillard at Wyandotte, in the viaduct. He gazed at the heavy steel beams that supported the train bridge. They'd jumped in front of and led to the demise of many vehicles. A series of pictures flashed through his mind. It was a collection he'd seen while working as a cadet in the traffic office.

There was a fatal motorcycle crash just before he became a cop. A high-speed pursuit that ended badly. Police had chased a man across the east side of the city. He probably thought he'd lost them as he flew down Wyandotte Street like a rocket, leaving them in his dust. Obviously, he didn't see the roadblock past the bend in the road where it descended into the viaduct.

He barely had time to brake when he saw the two cruisers that blocked the road. They estimated he hit the police car at eighty miles per hour. He'd almost made it home. He lived just around the corner, off Drouillard Road. The dead biker was identified as Daniel Gates, Donny's father.

A couple of right turns and Norm pulled into the plaza lot to pick up his business cards. After travelling extensively in his first two years of retirement, he'd written a book of short stories, snippets of his worldly adventures. People liked his writing style and the book sold well.

While he parked the car, he considered the idea of writing a crime novel to tell some of his cop stories. Maybe he could write about his years on the beat, and characters like Donny Gates.

He picked up the business cards and returned to his car. While slipping a few of the crisp new cards into his wallet he recalled the third time he arrested Gates. No surprise—he'd caught him breaching his parole again.

Norm was in the Drug Squad at the time and following up on a tip from one of his confidential informants who was trying to work a patch; trading information for consideration on his own outstanding drug charges.

The CI told Norm about a dealer on Drouillard Road where he bought cocaine. He only knew the dealer as Don, and said he met him at Yesterday's Tavern. The name didn't mean anything to Norm at the time, Gates never came to mind.

Acting on the informant's information, the drug cops set up surveillance at Yesterday's. Norm took the eye and sat in an undercover van, parked across the street from the tavern. The time for the deal was prearranged. He only had to sit and wait for his rat to show up. It was a hot summer night and the bar had their front doors wide open, offering Norm an unobstructed view of two guys playing pool inside.

Seeing cops doing stakeouts on television looks like fun. They sit in plain view, joking with each other and eating donuts. It's quite different in real life. First of all, the criminal element in a tight neighborhood like Drouillard spot police vehicles as easily as black jelly beans. Any strange vehicle in the hood, even if it's parked, raises suspicion. Unlike the TV cop shows, local police can rarely afford commercial vehicles or other conveyances that might blend in.

To have their vehicle go unnoticed, one of Norm's comrades drove and parked the van. He walked away appearing to leave the van empty. That minivan was equipped with heavily tinted windows and curtains in the back section, for complete seclusion. There was a lawn chair to sit on and Norm brought along a bottle of Pepsi to stay hydrated.

Being concealed in a closed, locked van is not fun in the heat of a Windsor summer. The engine can't be used so there is no air conditioning. Bringing something to drink and eat is not a problem but disposing of the food and beverages once they've passed through your system is another matter. Norm learned how to recycle soda pop by refilling the empty bottle. Having to go number two was not an option.

Like all druggies and their dealers, Norm's informant showed up late. He walked into the bar and talked to the men playing pool. Within minutes one of them headed to the front door. It was on the grey side of dusk when he paused under the light that shone down from the business' sign above the entrance. The man peered directly at the van—it felt like his stare was locked onto Norms, even though he was hidden from view.

The face was familiar, his eyes gave him away. It was Donny Gates. He turned and said something to his buddy who was still inside the tavern, then he walked north along Drouillard. Norm called out the action to his team members on the radio, their job was to follow the target to see where he stashed his dope.

While they asked for the suspect's description and direction of travel Norm watched the other pool player walk toward his van. He whispered to the others and then shut off the radio. Without hesitation the man approached the van and made a loop around it. He looked through all the windows and pressed his face up against the rear glass, trying to see inside. Norm was as quiet and as still as a rock.

The man turned away for a moment, looked up and down the street. Then he tried to open the driver and passenger doors. Sweat streamed down the sides of Norm's face, but he was afraid to move and didn't attempt to wipe it.

His heart pounded and he held his breath, fearing it could be heard outside. The guy took another look through the windshield, and then walked back to the bar. Norm gasped, as if he hadn't breathed in ten minutes. He was soaked with perspiration.

A few minutes later Gates returned and exchanged cocaine for money with the informant. As the CI left the bar, he scratched the top of his head. That was the prearranged signal indicating the deal had been made.

The Drug Squad converged on Yesterday's and arrested Gates for trafficking. Norm made his way to the cop shop to apply for a search warrant for the house where Gates had picked up the coke. It was his mother's home.

Eight

Bad Boys

Celine Charbot liked to party. She'd been a rebel from the time she was fourteen years old. Her mother tried in vain to rein her in but sympathized because she had acted in the same way at that age. Regardless, she didn't want to see Celine make the same mistakes she did.

She was a looker with a body most girls would kill for, and her face could have graced any fashion magazine. Since puberty, Celine looked older than she was, but her immaturity showed in her choice of men and her life decisions.

Bob Killen, Celine's stepfather, did his best to understand and discipline her, but he knew it was a battle he'd never win. She was just like her mother, who was only seventeen when Bob began dating her. Terri Charbot was the reason for his failed marriage. Addicted to her, he couldn't get enough.

Like her daughter, Terri was beautiful and attracted to bad boys. She shunned Bob at first because he was a cop. That didn't fit with her preferred lifestyle. Even though he wore the uniform of the Windsor Police, Bob was a rebel too. He had a hard time with the quasi-military structure of the police force and the strict rules that came with it.

He pushed the envelope and pissed off his superiors by letting his moustache, sideburns and hair grow longer than regulations allowed. He drank and partied along with his fellow cops but wore blinders when his under-aged girlfriend openly drank in public or smoked pot behind closed doors. Eventually, he chose Terri over his brothers in blue, and resigned.

Having seen the seedier side of life, Bob intervened in Celine's relationships more than once, scaring or chasing off the bad boys. She got pissed off and ran away from home several times, but usually returned on her own when she ran out of money or places to crash. That all stopped when she returned home one day and announced she was pregnant.

Terri had firsthand knowledge of what it was like to be a teenager and raise a child, but Celine rejected her advice, stating she could do it better. It wasn't long before she had another scrap with her mother and left home again. She hooked up with an old boyfriend and ran off with him to Calgary, where he'd been promised a job in the booming oil industry.

Bob and Terri were devastated, especially with a grandchild on the way. He reached out to police contacts, but with no news of Celine, they feared the worst. They worried for almost two months before they received the frenzied call. She'd lost the baby and Kenny had thrown her out. Apparently, she'd lied to him and said the child was his. Details weren't important, they wired their baby girl money for an airline ticket to come home.

After finding a decent job and having spent a year with her parents, Celine announced that she was moving in with a co-worker. It appeared that she might have grown up and was taking responsibility for her own life. Bob and Terri bought her stuff and helped with the move. His cop radar went off when he saw her apartment was in the scruffy part of Walkerville, it was bad enough she worked in a bar on Drouillard Road.

With Celine working at the bar and babysitting for one of Bob's old cop buddies, they barely saw their daughter. He ran into his former cop friend at a downtown bar. The former co-worker asked how Celine was doing. Responding to Bob's dumfounded look, the man said he thought they knew she wasn't babysitting any more. He had let her go.

His old buddy said that he and his wife had told Celine it was okay to have her boyfriend over after the kids went to bed. Then one night after she left their house, he found what he thought was cocaine on the coffee table. They didn't say anything at the time but made a point to get home early the next time Celine babysat. The cop was shocked when he recognized her boyfriend as Donny Gates.

Redness around Bob's neck spread to his cheeks and forehead.

His buddy dropped his eyes and said, "That's why I didn't say anything to you...I probably should've, but I was afraid you'd blow a gasket."

Bob's eyes bulged and veins popped out on his forehead. His old partner took a step back. Terri had been in a conversation with someone else, but saw that Bob was in distress. She went to his side and asked what was wrong. His mouth popped open, but no words escaped. He grabbed her by the arm and marched out of the bar.

On the way home, in the car, their discussion turned into a shouting match. Bob mistakenly compared Celine's stupidity to Terri's, saying she was a bad influence and terrible mother. She flipped out. Slaps became punches and one caught Bob on the side of his face. He pulled to the curb to avoid an accident and Terri bailed out of the car.

Eventually, Celine made nice with her mother and stepfather, usually with the ulterior motive of borrowing money. Bob was against helping as long as she was still involved with Gates. But Terri always gave in when Celine shed tears and helped her make up rent or car payments.

Terri may have been blinded by maternal love, but Bob knew better. His buddy told him that Celine and Gates were living together. That meant nothing but trouble as far as he was concerned. Having worked on Drouillard Road, Bob knew all about the Gates family and their criminal enterprises. He kept his mouth shut to avoid the inevitable scrap with Terri.

Nine

Project Punks

With his brand-new business cards in hand, Norm drove around the corner and parked in front of the furniture repair shop, another place he'd worked part time in retirement, whittling away his days.

As a child, he'd hung out in his Pepe's workshop learning from a handyman who could easily have been a carpenter. Norm loved the smell of freshly sawn lumber and the silky feel of a hand-sanded board.

He took building construction and architectural drafting in high school, and built a bar in his bedroom when he lived at home with his mother and siblings. Made from an old china cabinet and barn wood from the abandoned Walker Farms, he proudly displayed a collage of Playboy centerfolds under the glass top. He and his younger brother, by a year, kicked the youngest brother out of the room and into the hallway to make room for the bar.

After moving out on his own, Norm collected proper tools and built wood furniture on his apartment balcony. His next abode was a house. The basement became his workshop and the building site of larger projects like a tea cart and entertainment center. He expanded his skills by renovating and flipping various houses.

While in the neighborhood, Norm thought he'd pop in and say hey to Katrina, the woman who ran the shop. She'd moved from Calgary to start her own furniture refurbishing business, a talent that she'd inherited working with her father back home.

After seeing a newspaper article about her and the new business, Norm made a point of stopping in to introduce himself and offer his time as a part time apprentice.

It was a way for him to see if he still had an interest in woodworking, and to make a few extra bucks to supplement his retirement income. Norm chatted with Katrina for a while, they caught up while he checked out her latest restoration projects. The woman did amazing work, stuff that was way beyond his capabilities. She rejuvenated weathered antiques and gave them new life.

With one more stop to make, Norm left the shop and drove south on Walker Road. He looked at the empty lot that was previously a juice factory. The place he nearly died—where Johnny Eagle had pulled him out of the burning building.

He owed his life to the former arsonist and wondered for a second what happened to him after he moved away. Norm shook his head and remembered how his life had flashed through his mind before his passed out. Nope, he didn't miss the job.

Heading east on Seminole Street, he glanced up Central Avenue to see if he could catch a glimpse of the first house he'd bought. He made good money converting it into a rental, and then flipping it.

Passing the Hook & Ladder Club, he remembered the punks that lived in the city housing projects at the north end of Central; the Watsons and Stantons. The three Watson boys were all trouble-makers. Norm had arrested the two oldest on more than one occasion.

The Stanton boys were petty thieves who did B & E's like the Watsons, before they'd reached puberty. They once stole Norm's dog when he lived in the hood. Of course, they were too young and stupid to realize he might walk down the street looking for the animal. The projects were one of the reasons he moved out of the area.

Norm thought Ronny Stanton might turn out different, he once gave him a break by not arresting him on an outstanding warrant. It was an attempt to recruit Ronny as an informant, something that was next to impossible to do in the D. The kid seemed to be on board and promised to report back to Norm the next day. Then the midnight crew arrested Ronny for the outstanding warrant. He wouldn't talk to Norm after that.

Ronny admitted to the judge in court one day that he'd been committing crimes since he was eight years old. He had over thirty criminal convictions. Most were property related offences, but he had graduated to weapons and drug charges. At one of his hearings he begged for house arrest so he could stay home and take care of his ailing mother.

His brother Mickey was the worst of the two, and by far the king of criminals in the projects. Like Ronny, he racked up pages of criminal charges and spent as much time in jail as he did on the street.

He got into crack cocaine and his physical appearance suffered from heavy usage. Norm later read an article in the newspaper about Mickey trying to rob a bank downtown. It was a bizarre attempt. He lit up a cigarette and waited for the police to arrive.

In court he claimed he was mentally ill, that he wanted to go back to jail so he could receive treatment. Although he was a lot different than Ronny, they chose the same path in life. Norm believed Mickey was truly evil. He had cold black eyes. He never showed emotion and his smile was a sarcastic grin.

The Stanton brothers' paths were chosen for them, much like their extended family. Mickey had the same Charlie Manson eyes as his half-brother, Donny Gates. They had the same father—the biker who died fleeing the cops. It's no wonder they all hated the police. Maybe it also explained why the brothers with different mothers gravitated to Loretta Gates, the matriarch of Drouillard Road.

Ten

Living in Sin

Celine Charbot couldn't help herself. She was in love. The girl who had shared her apartment got tired of the all-night parties and moved out. Upon leaving she said she had no use for Donny Gates and that he was nothing but trouble. Celine shrugged it off. Donny had practically been living there, and he promised he'd help her with the rent.

In Celine's mind, Donny was a handsome man with a taught physique and cute butt. She interpreted his intense demeanor and dead eyes as pride and confidence. She knew of his previous incarceration for killing a man, but that didn't bother her. He led her to believe it was his best friend's fault and he was just along for the ride. The unknown and the element of danger gave her a tingling feeling inside, like butterflies.

When the two of them argued, she assumed it was natural. After all, she'd seen her mother and stepfather scrap plenty of times. It was how couples in love acted and responded to each other.

What bothered her about Donny was his family and friends. She couldn't comprehend his attachment and loyalty to a bunch of white trash that she considered losers. Celine didn't think he needed them. She wanted Donny all to herself.

The more time they spent together, the more they fought. His mind was usually elsewhere, or he was screwed up on booze, pills, or cocaine—sometimes a combination of all three. Celine didn't like what he'd become when he was stoned or intoxicated, but she partied right along-side him. She thought if she couldn't beat him, she'd join him. Celine enjoyed getting high.

They were living together when Donny got busted for dealing coke at Yesterday's Tavern on Drouillard Road. She waitressed there some nights, while he hung out and shot pool with his buddies from the hood.

She never considered what he did as dealing, as long as he kept her supplied with party material. Celine was more pissed at the cops than Donny when he got arrested. It was a bone of contention with her stepfather being a former police officer. She thought they were all assholes. Gates told her so.

She borrowed money from her parents to bail her man out of jail. She told them it was for car repairs. Her life was better when Donny was around. She was addicted to him, even more than the drugs they did daily. Celine didn't care that his mother got busted too, she had no use for the woman.

All good things must come to an end. Their relationship faced what was to be its final test. After she bailed Donny out of jail, he disappeared for the whole weekend. She called around to his usual haunts but was told he'd left or that they hadn't seen him. It was no surprise that his friends covered for him.

Celine had considered kicking him to the curb before, but she figured it was time to teach him that she meant business. He was as high as the sky when he finally returned home. Ignoring the suitcase she'd packed for him at the front door, he tossed a plastic bag of cocaine on the coffee table and then cozied up on the couch in front of it.

Donny had been on a three-day bender. Celine stared and gave him the silent treatment. She hadn't had a drop of booze all weekend. After a long look in the mirror that morning, she'd come to the conclusion it was time to clean up her act. Her life was going nowhere.

Donny's face was tight from the coke high, and his pupils nothing but black holes when he told Celine to get him a beer. She lost it and told him he was out of control with the booze and drugs.

She said she needed a break from it all, and him. He turned it around and said he knew it was coming and that he'd heard she'd been fucking around on him. Tears exploded and poured down her cheeks. She pointed to his duffle bag and the front door. He ignored her and leaned forward to open the bag of coke, but she tore it from his grasp.

White powder flew like snow in a winter's wind. Gates leaped up and grabbed Celine's arm, reaching for the bag with his other hand. She made sure it was empty and let it fall to the floor. Donny expelled a guttural roar that sounded like the growl of a pissed off grizzly bear.

He swung an open hand at Celine's face and almost connected. She pulled back and broke free. Her sudden move threw Donny off balance. He fell forward and landed on the coffee table, shattering the glass top. She ran into the bathroom, and tried to lock herself in. Within seconds he was there.

Celine flew backwards into the bathtub when the door crashed into her. Her hands and face took the impact, breaking two fingers and bloodying her nose. Her head bounced off the ceramic tile. The shower curtain did nothing to break her fall.

It was then that the love of her life attacked like a ravenous Hyena.

Eleven

911

Norm remembered the call for help like it was yesterday. Maybe it was because of the tone of the police officer's voice. His strained plea revealed the desperation and urgency of the situation. A domestic disturbance gone bad.

A man was locked in the bathroom with his girlfriend. Police believed she was badly injured. Neighbors complained of screaming, furniture breaking, and strange sounds like howling wounded animals.

The acting downtown Sergeant called for assistance, as he backed up the responding officer. Norm Strom was the Precinct Sergeant. He'd just left Headquarters after completing the mail run.

Two other cops ran from the building to their cruiser, but Norm had the jump on them, already headed in the direction of the call. Norm felt the tension in the acting Sergeant's labored words. He suggested the dispatcher start an ambulance to his location. He feared the woman was gravely injured. The man had blocked the bathroom door with his body to keep the police at bay. They thought the suspect had a weapon, possible a knife.

The cruiser's siren drowned out any further radio transmissions. Flashing headlights and emergency roof lights from the speeding police car behind him boosted Norm's adrenaline level even higher. It only took minutes to get to the scene of the disturbance, but it probably seemed longer to the cops who'd called for help.

Norm knew the feeling; he'd been in that position on more than one occasion. The sound of police sirens and knowing help was on the way was as reassuring as a loving mother's embrace.

It appeared as though a tornado had touched down in the apartment. Blood, shattered glass and broken furniture were strewn about the living room. Norm heard primeval sounds emanating from behind the bathroom door. The acting Sergeant told him Donny Gates was locked inside with his girlfriend. He feared the worst.

Gates was barely coherent. He'd made it clear he had a knife and would cut the first mother-fucker who came through the door. Celine was unresponsive. Gates said that she was drunk and had passed out. The cops knew what to do. They had to get into that room. They had to check on the woman. Their dilemma was how to do it safely.

While the initial responding officer tried to keep Gates talking at the door, the two Sergeants hatched a plan. Norm knew the other cop from working together in the Drug Squad. They both knew Donny Gates and what he was capable of.

The police had been in the apartment for almost twenty minutes. The law says that police can use lethal force if they fear for their own or someone else's life. Any armchair quarterback would suggest they shoot Gates through the bathroom door. However, the cops didn't know if he was truly armed or the condition of his girlfriend.

Their guts told them what needed to be done. Cops have to make decisions that will be judged by others who weren't there. They do what they must, knowing they'll have to live with their actions for the rest of their lives.

They considered the safety of both Donny and the woman inside the bathroom. Fearing she could be severely injured, or worse, they decided to force the door open and overtake Gates. The knife concerned them. Could they disarm him before he used it?

Their timing had to be perfect to knock Gates off balance and subdue him without anyone getting hurt. The young patrol officer nodded to the Sergeants. He was sure Gates was directly behind and up against the door. The two men shouldered the door with their combined weight of over four hundred pounds.

They got lucky. The force sent Donny backwards into the tub. He landed on top of Celine. The knife fell from his hand to the floor. The acting Sergeant was on Gates before he knew what happened. Donny was handcuffed and dragged out of the bathroom.

Norm stood there for a moment, dumbfounded. The room looked like a movie set in a horror film. The mirror, sink, and toilet were broken. The ceiling, walls, and floor were dripping with blood spatter. The air stunk of sulfur, sweat, and urine. The ravaged body in the bathtub made no sound. There was no movement or any signs of a living, breathing person.

Everyone said that Celine Charbot was a beautiful young woman with a great figure. That's not what Norm witnessed in the bloodied and butchered corpse. She was curled in a fetal position in a pool of her own blood. Her hair was matted and crimson-crusted, eyes closed. Her hands were clasped together like she just said her prayers and fell asleep for the night. That might have been the case if it wasn't for the gaping stab wounds all over her body.

Twelve

Circle of Life

Norm stopped for the traffic light on Pillette at Tecumseh Road. He looked south across the intersection to the commercial buildings. He remembered that one of them once housed the Sandwich East Police Department. That was before the township was annexed by Windsor. The building later housed a doctor's office, a magic shop, and a Chinese restaurant.

He was only a kid when he'd heard about a stabbing in the front doorway while the cops were out on patrol. It was one of life's oddities. Someone causing harm to another person at a place where the occupants were sworn to protect everyone. It was one of the reasons Norm became a cop, to help those wronged by others. He thought it was a noble thing to do.

His mind still searched for memories; Norm considered his career in policing. He did a lot of good and helped as many people as he could. There were good times and bad. Overall, he was proud of what he'd accomplished in his thirty-one years. He made the turn when the light changed, and smiled at himself in the mirror. It was funny, he thought, how he didn't miss the job.

A shiny new Windsor Police cruiser passed in the opposite direction. Norm didn't recognize the driver. He could have been the man hired to fill the void when he retired. Who knows? Everyone is replaceable. The fact remained that criminals would continue to do what they do and cops would continue to do what they do to stop them. Such is life.

Donny Gates was jarred awake by the shout of a guard. He'd slept through the wakeup buzzer and was late for the morning head count. Some convicts had trouble sleeping in prison, possibly because of a troubled conscious, but more likely because of the noisy environment. Neither was a problem for Gates. He slept like a baby.

He rubbed the crusty residue from his eyes with his fingertips and sat up in bed. A burly guard stared at him from the door, shaking his head. Donny did nothing to acknowledge his presence. He stared at the cold grey cement on the opposite side of his cell. The blank wall depicted a perfect picture of everything he had accomplished in life.

'Knock-Out'

One

Corktown

Like a lion stalking its prey, he hunkered down behind the mail box on the corner. To hunt in daylight was risky, but it was out of necessity. People were like sheep; he only needed to thin the herd and find the weak one. Traffic was favorably light, the perfect victim stopped for the signal.

Abigail Brown scanned the empty sidewalks and alcoves along Michigan Avenue and fondly recalled when Tiger Stadium loomed over the intersection at Trumball, in Corktown. The team's move and the city's bankruptcy were a double whammy to the once vibrant community. Azure sky crested the barren streetscape; perfect weather for the all-American past time.

The area got more than its fair share of burglaries, adding insult to injury. The two Detectives cruised the avenue with eyes wide open. They had a few suspects in mind. The brass called it directed patrol; dreaming police would stumble across a burglary in progress.

It was wishful thinking at best, but the public needed assurance the Detroit Police were on the job. In reality, the cops were there to keep the neighbourhood safe for gamblers at Motor City Casino.

Yuppies moved into the area to be near new companies taking advantage of rock-bottom real estate prices. Restaurants and bars appeared, catering to their hungry and thirsty neighbours. Brown's nostrils caught the aroma of smoked meat when they stopped for a traffic light. Slow's Barbeque was geared up for lunch. Her mouth salivated at the thought of a pulled pork sandwich.

She glanced at her partner admiring his profile and physique. Everything about Dwayne Johnson was perfect. She'd been working robberies and burglaries with him for almost two years. More handsome than the actor of the same name and with the same athletic build, the other cops called him The Rock.

Her partner focussed on a car facing them, across the intersection. A black man crossed the street in front it, his gaze locked on the female driver. When he slipped a hand under the front of his shirt they instinctively reached for their guns at the same time. Abigail's heart leapt in her chest.

The gunman went to the driver's side, reached in through the open window, and put the gun to the woman's temple. He grabbed her by the hair and opened the door. She screamed for her life. The assailant yelled something about killing her while he tried to pull her out of the car, but she was caught in her seat belt.

They were in an unmarked Chevy. Johnson punched the accelerator and made a beeline for the crime in progress. The culprit saw them coming and he fired two shots in their direction. One bullet skipped off the hood of their car.

The perp ran around the front of the victim's car, retreating the way he came. Dwayne had a death grip on the steering wheel and he didn't let up off the accelerator. Abigail thought he would run the assailant down.

Adrenaline pumped through her veins. She raised her weapon and considered returning fire out the open window. It wasn't clear what happened next. The victim either panicked or tried to hit her attacker with her car. She accelerated and veered right, forcing Johnson to go left. The scene unfolded in slow motion. The gunman leapt like a kangaroo and narrowly avoided becoming a dirt bag sandwich.

The victim's car ploughed into Abigail's door and both vehicles rolled up onto the sidewalk. Abigail tried to exit the car and pursue the suspect, but the door was jammed. Her heart pounded inside her chest as if it was trying to escape a locked box.

Brown turned to Johnson, but he was already out and sprinting after the suspect. She reached for the portable radio, but it had fallen off the front seat during the collision. By the time she scrambled out the driver's side of the car her partner had disappeared into an alley.

Abigail glanced back at the victim, she waved her off and pointed in the direction of the foot chase. She ran after them. The alley was empty when Detective Brown got to it, but she heard two gun shots and her partner call out, "Police!"

She jumped a low fence and ran through someone's back yard, in the direction of his voice. Tunnel vision had kicked in by the time she rounded the corner of the house. The Detective heard a dog, but didn't see it until her right foot was in its mouth.

Her leg didn't follow her body when she made the turn, the knee gave out and she crashed down on top of the dog. It was bedlam. The animal yelped, she shrieked, her partner shouted, and gunfire erupted. Pain ran amuck through her body.

His pistol aimed at the perp, Johnson crouched behind a porch for cover. When he saw Brown hit the ground, exposed and in the open, he reached for her. Time stood still. Abigail thought she was in a horror movie. Blood spewed from Dwayne's neck. Her reflexes took over and she discharged her weapon repeatedly until the gunman disappeared.

The mutt whimpered. Her partner moaned. She blacked out.

Six Months Later...

Two

Roasted Chestnuts

Abigail Brown hated winter. Especially the damp and bitter Michigan cold that came in the middle of January. The temperature hovered around freezing, but the chill factor took another ten degrees off the Fahrenheit scale. She parked the unmarked Chevy behind the police cruiser, in the 3000 block of Charlevoix. Yellow crime scene tape blocked the entrance to the driveway.

With a closed hand to her mouth, she blew hot air to warm her fingers. She tried to note the arrival time in her ledger, but the thick ink refused to flow. She gave the pen a good shake as she glanced around the barren east side neighbourhood, wondering how it had looked in the city's heyday. The aluminium-sided, storey and a half house was flanked by empty lots. The opposite side of the street was nothing but a field for the entire length of the block.

The homicide rate from the previous year entered her mind. It had broken three hundred. Even at almost one per day, it was nowhere near the seven hundred and fourteen back in 1974 when Detroit earned the title of Murder City. That was well before her time. She tightened her Ann Taylor cashmere scarf and tried to imagine that the snow outside the car was white sand on a sunny beach, in Jamaica.

Force of habit caused Abigail to check her reflection in the rear-view mirror. The makeup was almost perfect, but the cold chapped her lips. She pressed them together to smooth the lipstick, then checked her hair. Not that it mattered, the wind would surely wreak havoc on her loose brown curls. Her eyes, usually chestnut brown, picked up the muted grey in the winter sky.

Arctic wind from a polar vortex ripped the car door from her hand and pulled her out into the street. Holding onto the car to for balance, Abigail checked her footing on the icy pavement and inched to the front of the house. Traction was better on the un-shovelled sidewalk. The aluminum door flew open when she reached the top step of the porch. Luckily, she wasn't standing in its way as it crashed against the wall.

"Sorry, I couldn't hang on to it." A uniformed officer stood inside the doorway.

"What are you doing in my crime scene, McCarthy?"

"It's fucking freezing outside and the heat don't work in my piece of shit cruiser, Detective Brown. Besides, I asked the dead guy. He doesn't mind. Crime Scene Services said their battery's dead and they're waiting for a jump. Don't worry, I didn't touch anything."

She stepped inside and closed the interior door.

"What've you got, Mick?"

His uniform was wrinkled, and what appeared to be a coffee stain sullied his shirt. There were only a few threads of red left in his thin, receding grey hair. McCarthy was one of the few remaining old-school Irish cops on the job.

Abigail knew him from the local bar they frequented. Mick should have owned shares in the place. He fumbled for his notebook. Although he said he didn't touch anything, there was a trail of melted snow on the carpet, apparently leading to the bathroom. He caught the Detective looking at the floor.

"What was I supposed to do, piss off the porch?"

"Not in this weather from what I've heard you can't afford the shrinkage."

He grunted.

"Aye, guess I can't argue that. Guy down the street came over to borrow some tools. Name's Manfred Fisher. He says the front door wasn't locked and he walked in and found the Vic like that. Detective Brown...meet Alberto Molina."

"Any signs of forced entry?"

"Not that I could see...while I wasn't contaminating your crime scene."

Detective Brown surveyed the room. Molina sat in a recliner, on the opposite side of the living room, facing the television. It was on a table three feet to the right of the front door.

"Was the TV on when you came in?"

"I shut it off. Some idiots on Jerry Springer were screaming at each other."

"What else didn't you touch, besides yourself?"

Mick ignored the question.

"Neighbour says Molina lived alone...had a wife and kid who left years ago. He was on some kind of disability pension. Mostly kept to himself. He's got a good set of mechanic's tools in the back room and Fisher borrowed them from time to time. Must've been a pervert to have his balls blown off like that."

"Is that your expert opinion, officer?"

"Just sayin." He pointed to the hole in the victim's chest.

"Guess that one finished him."

"Appears he bled a lot first. The shooter wanted him to suffer a while."

The street cop cringed.

"Poor bastard."

Abigail leaned in for a closer look at the wounds. She'd seen her share of human carnage between Afghanistan and the mean streets of Detroit.

Mick cleared his throat.

"Are you done with me, Detective? I haven't had my lunch yet."

"You can canvass the neighbourhood and see if anyone saw or heard anything that might help us."

"In this area? Even if they did, they're not going to tell me about it."

"Use your Irish charm. Maybe some lonely old woman will make you a sandwich or bowl of soup while you're *doing your fucking job.*"

McCarthy turned to leave, mumbled something about her foul mouth and roasted chestnuts over an open fire. Brown pulled a pair of rubber gloves from her pocket and shed the Jacqueline Smith leather coat.

She put her notebook on the table beside the door. A set of car keys was splayed over an open pack of Juicy Fruit. A glance out the window at the driveway, revealed no car parked there or on the street.

The Detective scanned the room, a thousand things ran through her mind; policy, procedure, investigative techniques, protocol, forensics, her new captain. Had he given her too much credit, working a case on her own, or was it because nobody wanted to work with her after the shooting?

She stood in front of the victim; Abigail examined him from head to toe. Any normal person would be freaked out, sharing quality alone time with decomposing human remains. It was part of her job. It wasn't dead people who bothered her, it was those who'd been gravely injured and cried out for help. That's what she really dreaded, especially if it was someone she knew.

Brown continued her examination. It was hard to miss the dark red goo in the victim's lap. It appeared that he had been shot point blank in the crotch. Small chunks and pieces of flesh were all that remained of his testicles, laying in a pool of coagulated blood. His grey jogging pants were soaked from his bodily fluids. Stippling from the gunshot was visible around both wounds.

He'd been shot twice with a large calibre bullet, while sitting in his chair.

The lack of blood on his abdomen led the Detective to believe that the victim was shot in the groin first, while his heart was still pumping. The injury would have incapacitated him while he waited for the kill shot. She wondered what Molina did to deserve such a slow and painful death.

She took a step back and looked over the victim again, poked her head around both sides of the chair, but couldn't find any shell casings. Under the end table, something caught her eye. It was the TV remote. Had he been watching the tube when the intruder entered his home and shot him?

Her brain in high gear, she scribbled notes to describe the victim and his wounds. He was Hispanic—a bit unusual for the predominately black neighbourhood, late forties or early fifties. Balding, no facial hair, Molina was of medium height and build, carrying a good-sized spare tire around his waist. He was dressed in an old Adidas track suit and thick grey work socks.

Methodically, she moved from the body to the chair and table next to it. She catalogued everything, and paused from time to time to take photographs with her phone. It's not that she didn't trust the crime scene techs. Abigail liked to compare her work to theirs for different perspectives. In need of an evidence bag, she checked the time and wondered when CSS would arrive.

Three

Double Trouble

The sound of a car door out front caught Detective Brown's attention. From her crouched position near the television, she stood and turned at the same time. There was no pain in her knee. The replacement surgery had gone well. The doctor recommended the procedure be done after removing the bullet from her thigh. Two birds with one scalpel, he'd said.

The chunk of lead hadn't hit anything vital, but the cartilage in her knee was shredded from basketball, war injuries, and the lack of proper treatment. The time in the hospital and rehab was a blur. She was happy to be back at work.

Lieutenant Michael Robinson met the Detective at the front door.

"Everything under control, Abigail?"

"Hey, LT, just waiting on CSS. Any idea where the fuck they are?"

Her boss grimaced.

"They're over on the west side, Tintenelli and Walker have a sex crime."

Robinson thought everything was a sex crime. He'd recently been promoted from that unit. He stood wide-eyed, gawking at the man with crimson holes in his chest and crotch. His dark chocolate skin was sallow from frigid winter air, and his face scrunched as always when he spoke.

"What happened to his...?"

Brown mimicked a gun and pointed to the victim's lap.

"His frank and beans? A large calibre bullet blew them to hell."

"God almighty, what did this sinner do to have such a vile act done to him? You could show a little more respect, Abigail. And your language...you know how I feel about that."

A religious man, his time in sex crimes almost drove him over the edge. Small in frame and stature he resembled a banker more than a cop. He'd hoped to move to and retire from Financial Crimes, but they promoted Robinson and sent him to Major Crimes. It was the common theme of the previous regime, ignore problems by bumping them up a grade.

Abigail eyed her boss.

"I thought CSS was coming here. When did Boxer and Two-Tone get their DB?"

The Lieutenant was fixated on the body. He mumbled something to himself while he signed the cross.

"Detectives Tintenelli and Walker got theirs right after yours. CSS called the office to say they had a dead battery, so they went to the garage to give them a jump."

"Shit! They jacked forensics before they got to me. That's just great LT, are you calling in another CSS team?"

Robinson's pallor wasn't much better than the dead man. He broke from his trance.

"The Captain reprimanded me for allowing frivolous overtime, there's no money in the budget for it. Is there is anything else you need."

"A partner would be nice. And since the other two *Dicks* are busy, maybe some uniforms to help McCarthy with the canvass?"

He cringed at every bad word that left her lips. It was a bad habit she'd picked up in the military but something she usually had under control, except when she was stressed or pissed off, or wanted to drive home a point.

"The Patrol Division's shorthanded too, Abigail. McCarthy, does he have drinking problem?"

"That's funny." She said. "He has a life problem. Alcohol helps him cope."

Robinson shook his head.

"My hands are tied, Abigail. They won't give us any more investigative personnel; every division is shorthanded. We have an odd number in the office, you have to work solo. The Captain thought about shuffling partners when you came on board, but you know how some feel about you. You know...after the shooting."

Brown squared off and faced her Lieutenant.

"Yeah, I've heard they say a lot of shit behind my back, but nothing to my face. They seem to forget I lost my partner, and took a bullet too."

"I'm sorry, Abigail, you know I don't indulge in gossip. Don't fret young lady, the righteous will prevail. I have to call the Captain. He'll want to know about these two homicides. I hope we don't have a serial."

Like the Devil himself had spooked him, Robinson turned to leave. Brown caught his elbow as he reached for the door. "Serial? What do mean? What've they got?"

"Their victim was stabbed to death...sounds like it's sexually motivated."

Her chest tightened.

"That doesn't sound like a coincidence—different weapon, but a similar MO?"

The Lieutenant glanced back at her and shrugged on his way out the door.

"I'll see if I can scrounge up some uniforms for you."

Detective Brown closed the door behind him, stood there in thought and gazed out the window. *Great. Walker and Tintenelli will want to take this over, call it a serial just to suck up to the Captain and make themselves look important.* She turned and stared at the victim. *I guess neither of us are going anywhere...so tell me what happened to you, Mr. Molina.*

Robinson honked as he left the curb. The Medical Examiner pulled into the vacated spot. Abigail thought she really didn't need an opinion for cause of death, it was a no-brainer. What she was more interested in knowing if their office had come across any similar dead bodies in the county.

Four

Hammer Time

"Here's one now, are ya ready?"

The shorter of the two men, known as D, answered.

"It's recordin, don't fugit ta smile, Dawg."

The size and stature of a big brother, C Dawg mugged for the camera, and then headed in the direction of the woman carrying a load of shopping bags. She was walking to a red minivan parked on the street. Like most white women who meet young black men on a sidewalk in the City of Detroit, she avoided eye contact with the young dude in the black hoodie and ball cap.

As C Dawg passed her, he threw a roundhouse punch. The blow landed under her chin and lifted the petite woman off her feet. Her head snapped back and her knees buckled, dropping her to the sidewalk. Arms, legs, and groceries splayed across the cement as if she'd been struck by lightning.

The thug spun around to face the camera, flung his arms in the air like he held the championship belt for a heavyweight title fight. Someone yelled from across the street. C Dawg bolted, trying to catch D, who was already sprinting away.

They both ducked into an alley a few blocks away. Trying to catch his breath, C Dawg turned to D,

"Ya see dat? Almost took her head off...went down like a rag doll. K.O!"

D thumbed the buttons on his phone.

"That was crazy, Dawg. And now for the instant replay?"

The alley was empty and dark, the video lit their faces. As if watching their favourite sitcom, they laughed out loud.

C Dawg beamed.

"That'll get me in the game...gonna be da champ, you see."

D still breathed heavily.

"Not yet, homie, 666 still da man. He as bad as the devil for sure."

"Yah, but they be readin bout the Thumper...how 666 is just a humper, going down the dumper. He laughed at himself. Hows you like my rap, D Man?"

D reached out and flipped up the brim of C Dawg's ball cap.

"You cool as ice, man. Hey maybe dat be my game name. Iceman...or just Ice, Like Ice T."

C Dawg punched D on the arm.

"Sure thing, water boy. Hit replay again."

Five

Say Uncle

A post-it note on the stack of files that someone had dumped on Abigail's desk fluttered from the gush of warm air blowing from the ceiling vent. She recognized the Captain's scribbling, *see Chief Jackson ASAP.*

The Detective took the note, stuck it on her phone, and gawked at the pile of folders. The cases were all hers and Johnson's old investigations. The ones they'd worked on in Burglary prior to the shooting.

The button for the Captain's extension was lit up on her phone. *Perfect, he's in his office.* Abigail planned on devouring the Greek salad she'd picked up on the way in, but the mountain of work in front of her killed any appetite. She pulled the gun holster off her belt and tucked it in the desk drawer.

Lieutenant Robinson saw her heading for the Captain's office and pretended he was engrossed in his work. Her boss hung up the phone when she got to his door. David Baldwin removed his reading glasses and waved her in.

"Detective Brown, did you see the Chief yet?"

"No, sir, I thought I'd see you first and ask you about..."

"What did my note say? He's the top dog, see me when you get back."

She wanted to ask about the files on her desk, but knew better. Baldwin was a prick, recently promoted from Internal Affairs, and on his way up the ladder. She thought he was handsome for a white man, but the arrogance that oozed from his pores was so thick she almost gagged on it.

"Yes, sir." Brown answered, keeping her thoughts to myself.

The Chief's office was on the top floor, with a view of the Detroit River and across the water, the City of Windsor. Brown had only been in the office once before, when she returned to work after the shooting. The secretary told her to go right in, that she was expected.

Her uncle Chuck looked small, sitting behind his huge walnut desk. She'd called him that from an early age. He partnered with her real uncle, Bill Myers, the man who raised her.

"Abigail, come in."

He stood smiling with his arms outstretched.

"Come give an old man some love."

They embraced. At first, she thought he'd shrunk, but her high heels gave her two inches on him. He wore Old Spice as long as she'd known him, the scent comforted her and reminded her of childhood. He sat down and motioned for her to take one of the overstuffed leather chairs in front of his desk.

"Chief, Captain Baldwin said you wanted to see me?"

"Abigail, you know you can call me Uncle Chuck when we're alone."

"I know, but it doesn't sound respectful. Besides, you've earned the title and I like acknowledging that. I'm proud of you."

"How's my old partner? I haven't seen him in a while."

Brown glanced over the cluster of gold stars on his right shoulder, to Canada, and mused about a man she knew there.

"He's well. Has his own little kingdom over there at Comerica Park and thinks he's pretty important. But mostly he sits on his fat ass pretending to monitor security cameras while he scratches his balls and watches the games."

The Chief offered up a deep belly laugh.

"Always loved your vocabulary, Abigail. There are too many ass-kissers around here who talk to me like I'm royalty. Tell the old codger I'll try to get there next season, maybe the Tigers will do better this year. I haven't seen you since your transfer. How are you getting along in your new office?"

"Besides the usual bullshit from the old boy's club, I'm making a go of it. Just picked up an interesting homicide today and it might even be a serial."

He leaned back in his chair, folded his arms.

"Your Captain told me about it, said Tintenelli and Walker were lead. Didn't mention you being part of it."

"Doesn't surprise me, it's like I don't exist in his eyes. He dumped a pile of my old files from Burglary on me. Doesn't look like anyone touched them while I was gone."

The Chief leaned in, frowned. The thick worry lines that ran from the bridge of his nose along the front of his bald head resembled ripples on a sandy beach.

"You know what I think of Baldwin. He made a name for himself taking down the former Mayor's dirty cops. A whistleblower got him that far. He's a bean counter at best. Unfortunately, he got bumped up before I had any say in it.

The old regime left this place in shambles. I don't have enough cars or personnel to cover the streets. Private companies have donated some vehicles, but who knows if or when anyone will ever get a pay raise. Wages are frozen.

Truth is lots of cops are doing twice the work with half the resources. I'm sorry your generation is caught up in it and paying for our mistakes."

Abigail reached across his desktop, and took his big hands in hers.

"I don't envy you. Given some time, I'm sure you'll make things better around here. Is there something in particular you wanted to see me about?"

He squeezed her slender hands with his.

"It's the only way I get to see you. I wouldn't want the old boys club to get their backs up if I showed up in your office."

"Oh, I'm sure the word will get out that I was up here kissing your ass. Don't worry, I can handle any flak."

"Do you want me to ask your Captain where you stand in these recent murder cases?"

"No, that will only make things worse. I'll manage—always have and always will. Something I learned from you and dad; when the going gets tough, the tough get tougher.

The Chief sat back in his chair and laughed, his baritone voice carried across the room and echoed off the windows. His phone rang and he checked the display.

"I have to take this. Can you let yourself out? It was great to see you. Tell your old man I said hey."

Abigail stood and mocked a salute. He smiled and returned the same, then answered his phone. She took another quick glance out the window at the frozen Canadian coastline, and left.

Six

Plenty of Fish

Norm Strom stared at the majestic image on his computer screen, Machu Picchu. The sacred Inca village that rested high in the Andes mountains was on his bucket list, and the planned visit was only days away. He'd fly into Lima, Peru and start his South American adventure. The seasons being opposite south of the equator, made it the perfect winter destination.

From Lima, he hoped to see the ancient ruins of Caral, in the northern part of the country. He planned to use Cusco as a base, and would acclimatize to the high altitude before taking the train up to Agua Calientes, and eventually the sacred valley and Machu Picchu.

Strom switched from one screen to another, checking travel destination and reservations hoping to satisfy his wanderlust itch. He smiled when he opened his email and saw his new friend had dropped him a line. Being single, Norm thought it might be a good idea to use his dating site, Plenty of Fish, to meet someone in Lima, Peru.

It was a longshot, but he figured it was a good way to meet a local who just might be willing to act as a tour guide while he was in town. His buddies laughed when he hatched the idea, but he had the last laugh when he landed a fish. The Peruvian princess looked hot online, and she agreed to show Norm around her city.

He checked the dating site to see if he had any other new messages. Pictures of new fish popped up on his screen, one a pretty black woman from Detroit. He'd barely glanced at her picture when he thought of Abigail Brown. Norm wondered why the two of them weren't together.

They'd met through Bill Meyers, back when he and Strom were on the job and they took down Jimmy Flynn. The Detroit cop's niece, Abigail, was fresh out of college and looking to travel Europe for the summer. Norm gave her advice on must see places in Italy and France.

They flirted during the conversations, but Norm was married at the time. He bumped into her again years later, when he visited Meyers at Tiger Stadium. The comfortable relationship picked up right where it left off, and they hooked up after Norm's divorce.

Their timing sucked. Either their jobs or other short-term relationships kept them apart. A few dates and a wonderful weekend at a B & B in Niagara-on-the-Lake were all they managed. Norm heard about her taking a bullet on the job and intended to visit her in the hospital, but he got hung up in northern British Columbia helping the Mounties find a missing woman.

He scanned the faces on the dating site again. Too bad Abigail wasn't a member, he could send her a provocative email. She'd scoffed when he mentioned the site to her, said she'd rather be alone. Norm was different, he didn't like flying solo. He stared through the screen, thought maybe he would call Bill Meyers and see what his niece was up to.

A message from the dating site popped up, but he couldn't stop thinking about his favorite hot chocolate. That's what he called Abigail Brown. He eyed his cell phone on the desk. It couldn't hurt to call, but what was the use, he was leaving the country in a few days. His timing was terrible. Norm banged off a response to the Peruvian Princess and asked how they should meet on his arrival.

Seven

Black Olives

The Captain wasn't in his office when she got back. Her Lieutenant tossed an explanation her way.

"He's in a meeting the rest of the afternoon. He said he expects your homicide report on his desk by morning. Did you have a chance to look at those old files I left on your desk?"

"You're shitting me, right? I've been back to work less than a week. I spent my first day filling out compensation forms and qualifying at the range. Then after getting up to speed up on new policies and procedures, I caught the Molina homicide. It looks like no one's touched those files since I left, and now you're in a fricking hurry to clear them?"

Robinson scrunched his face—his best attempt at a scowl.

"Are you done whining...and cursing, Detective Brown?"

Before she could answer, he continued.

"You know we're understaffed. It's not my fault you weren't replaced and your cases sat idle while you were gone. I'm sure you're aware of how excrement flows downhill around here. The Commander dumps on the Captain, who dumps on me, and I dump on you. Those open files affect our clearance rating. The Captain's all over me to crack down and get results."

Brown stood there and stared at him for a moment. He was like Teflon—nothing stuck to him. The perfect middleman who knew how to appease his superiors and displease his subordinates all at the same time. Thinking for a second that she deserved some credit for not using the f word, she turned, and walked back to her cubicle.

Three feet above her desk amber light beamed through the window. It changed the perspective of the abstract water color that hung on the wall. *Too bad I'm not nine feet tall so I could see outside the building.* The windows sat high in the walls for security reasons. Thinking the stack of files might disappear if ignored, she relocated it to the top of her filing cabinet.

Work the homicide, she told herself. Maybe it would help her forget about all the work she and Dwayne did on those case files. He was the best partner she'd ever had. Abigail flipped through her notebook; the pages became a series of photos.

They'd done good police work, and a great partnership. There was only one slip. They got drunk after solving a big case and had sex. They both knew it was a mistake, but that didn't mean her loins didn't scream every time she looked at The Rock. He was so hot.

She thought about her man friend across the border, in Windsor. She hadn't seen Norm Strom in almost a year. Her uncle told her that his Canadian friend was enjoying his retirement, and said something about him rescuing a woman and catching a serial killer. He was the only white man who turned her on. It was his kind blue eyes, sexy smile, and laid-back attitude.

Brown found herself smiling. *I need to get laid. Focus, Abigail.* She logged into her computer and brought up the Molino file. After verifying the original call with the notes she'd made, Abigail started her supplementary report. The file showed Tintenelli and Walker as lead investigators. *Assholes!*

Her cellphone buzzed. It was her reminder to pick up the dry cleaning on the way home. She opened the photographs from the crime scene file and forwarded them to her own computer. The aroma of fermenting Greek salad filled the air over her desk like feta-scented perfume. She picked at the cucumbers and black olives while the photos popped open on the display screen.

When the download was complete, she sent a text to the forensic technician, requesting they forward their photos to her email. That gave her a chance to peruse them before they were attached to the hard copy case file, and sent into the hands of Walker and Tintenelli.

She perused her own photos one by one, chased a black olive with the plastic fork. Her appetite waned when she clicked on the photo of the victim's mutilated testicles. Abigail dropped the utensil into her salad and tossed the container into the trash can.

The dynamic duo walked into the outer office, she pretended not to seem them. They went directly to the LT's office and engaged in a three-way conversation. Five minutes passed and her phone rang. Robinson summoned her to his office. She faked another phone call and shuffled paper around on her desk for another five minutes, just to piss them off.

Her male co-workers occupied the only two chairs in front of the LT's desk so she stood in the doorway. One offered a half nod, and the other openly smirked and avoided eye contact with Brown. Jamal Walker was a former linebacker who'd been invited to a Lion's training camp, but couldn't cut the mustard. Joseph Tintenelli grew up in Grosse Point, he was Italian to the bone.

Abigail ignored them both and gave her attention to the Lieutenant.

"Detective Brown, these two are taking the lead on both of today's murders, but we'll need your keen eye and valuable input."

She listened, thinking, *Yeah, in other words you want me to do your typing and fetch coffee.* Abigail knew that any argument was a waste of time.

"I've got CSS sending in the crime scene photos now and I'm working on my report."

Robinson responded. "Good. Get your victim up on the board in the project room, and file your report with me before end of shift. I don't need you clocking any overtime on this unless we need you to run down a lead. Stay available and leave your phone on."

On her way out someone in the peanut gallery mumbled something, but she ignored it and headed for the ladies room. Her neck and forehead felt warm, frustration and anger made her blood boil and she'd forgotten she had to pee. Abigail sat quietly in the stall, took a couple of deep breaths to relax and regain her composure.

The tap water was ice-cold, pumped directly from the river. Abigail looked in the mirror, and fretted over her rosy cheeks. She took a few more minutes, and thought about that weekend getaway with her white knight.

Eight

Hit & Run

The first forty-eight hours of the two sexually motivated homicides were a bust. Detectives Walker and Tintenelli pretended to chase down important leads with each new day. Detective Brown was left behind in the office most of the time, to catalogue statements, notes, and evidence in the murder book.

As days became weeks all the investigators in the office took on new cases. Crime didn't sleep in the Murder City. There were drive-by shootings and stabbings to investigate, as well as a string of violent assaults. Abigail wasn't the least bit surprised when they assigned her a case from the 'Hit & Run' file.

Detroit Police received a handful of complaints about random victims attacked without provocation on the street. The file made its way to Major Crimes because one victim succumbed to her injuries. The case became a homicide investigation. Abigail wasn't sure what to make of the sporadic assaults. But she found similar incidents in the old cases she'd worked with Dwayne Johnson.

Abigail was no slouch at gathering information or research. During her tour in Afghanistan she'd worked as an Analyst for Army Intelligence. Police had none of the fancy equipment the military used, but she gained valuable experience in geographic and criminal profiling.

To bolster the suspicion she had about the random vicious assaults, she contacted one of her army buddies in New York. She knew the two major cities shared core problems, and her friend confirmed her hunch. According to the Big Apple connection, there was a new game in town called, 'knock-out.'

Gang bangers and street hoods had found a new way to amuse themselves on the mean streets of the big city. There were different versions of the game, but in most cases young assailants attacked unaware pedestrians. They sucker-punched their victims, the ultimate goal being to knock the person out cold. It appeared to Abigail that the game had caught on in Detroit.

After thanking her war buddy for the information, and agreeing they should get together soon, she felt angst. Like most, she did stupid things as a kid, but knocking someone unconscious on the street? It was sheer insanity. Her source told her that gang bangers used the game as either a form of initiation, or to raise their status.

Old Man Winter knocked on her office window. Abigail looked up at the sound of sleet pelting the tempered glass. It was the end of February, and the frigid weather didn't usually break until late March. Her mind saw palm trees blowing in an ocean breeze, while her eyes scanned witness statements looking for any kind of a suspect link. A Caribbean getaway would be great, she was in dire need of a real vacation.

She took to posting the victim's pictures on the bare wall opposite her window. Her request for a corkboard was denied because of budget restraints. The collage of human tragedy hung in stark contrast to the lone piece of abstract art in the room. The victims had nothing in common; not race or color, gender or age. Abigail noted similarities in the time and location of the attacks. Most happened in broad daylight, and all were in the downtown core.

Detective Brown studied the geography and made a note to call the gang squad in the morning. She wanted to know whose turf saw the most assaults. Her stomach growled. She looked at her wristwatch and up at the black curtain that cloaked the outside of her window. It was well past quitting time. The files would still be there in the morning. Abigail locked her desk and was about to shut down her computer when she noticed a new email.

It was from her friend across the border, Norm Strom. The time stamp said three in the morning. She figured he was either out of the country in a different time zone or drunk typing. The email was brief. He missed her, and they should get together. Abigail thought about responding, but decided to wait until she got home.

The aroma of fresh-baked bread wafted into her car through the air vents. She eyed the Little Caesar's Pizza on the corner. She only stopped for the traffic light, but pangs of hunger forced her hand. Abigail picked up a large salad and a bag of garlic-parmesan bread sticks.

Her apartment seemed bigger and emptier every time she walked through the door. Maybe it was time for some new furniture, or a makeover. The black and white on grey seemed crisp and cool when she bought it, but time had given it a clinical look that proved depressing.

After dropping her keys and dinner on the hall table, she hung her faux leather trench coat in the closet. Abigail peeled off her knee-high boots. She cringed at the salt stains that soaked into the suede, but it felt good to be free of the heels.

She removed her blazer. Famished, she grabbed the food and made a beeline for the kitchen counter. She pulled a part bottle of chardonnay from the fridge and poured a glass with one hand, while she removed dinner from the bag with the other. Abigail was not ladylike when craving sustenance, she filled her mouth with fresh bread and gulped wine while still chewing.

Toting her glass, she made her way to the stereo and turned on the CD player. The cartridge held a smooth jazz collection of female artists. Barbara Krall was first up. Abigail killed half the wine in two big gulps. She slid onto a kitchen stool and got serious with her dinner.

Dismayed that she couldn't squeeze a few more drops from the empty bottle, she contemplated opening another. She savoured the last mouthful of chardonnay, took note of the hints of American Oak from the barrel. It paired perfectly with the remaining crumbs of parmesan that lingered in her mouth.

The Celtic overtones of Lorena McKennitt caught her ear. Her white knight had introduced her to the Canadian singer. She was a native of Stratford, a Shakespearean town in Southern Ontario that Norm favoured and promised to take her to someday. The phone rang and her heart skipped a beat. She recognized Uncle Bill's number on the call display.

Nine

Breakfast Serial

Dark surrounded the glassed enclosed lobby of her apartment building. Like a fish in an aquarium, Abigail swung her arms and stretched her legs to get blood flowing to her extremities and to loosen taut muscles.

She didn't like the short winter days and lack of sunshine that came with them, but early morning runs were invigorating. They put her in the right frame of mind to handle the day ahead.

Her breath appeared and disappeared like the bursts of steam that spewed from manhole covers along the street. The city was quiet, mostly asleep. It hadn't snowed in weeks, but the sidewalks held a fine white powder. Her shoes squeaked when they pressed into it—the sound echoing off the buildings on either side.

Abigail Brown loved running. She didn't mind how the frigid air burned her lungs; it made her feel alive. She settled into a comfortable pace, feeling confident her new knee was better than ever. The marvels of medical science saved her. She was afraid she'd be crippled for life. Traffic lights the next several blocks changed to green in unison, nothing but open road lay ahead.

Her breathing synced with her strides. Abigail thought about her outstanding cases and mentally planned the day ahead. The bitter cold nipped at the nape of her neck and she adjusted her scarf. A poster in the travel agency window advertised a Caribbean cruise line. It was a nice thought, but perhaps some other time.

Azure water, white sand, and palms swaying in the breeze; born in Jamaica that scene had been etched in her mind since childhood. Her parents were blurry like ghosts from her past. She wasn't old enough to remember. Uncle Bill told her they were in heaven. She later discovered they'd been murdered, under very sketchy circumstances.

Abigail was sent to America, where her mother's brother and his wife raised her. Uncle Bill was a cop in Detroit and she followed in his footsteps. The only mother she really knew, her Aunt Martha, died of breast cancer when she was in high school.

Detective Brown's phone was ringing when she walked into her office. She was surprised by the call. It was early, and barely anyone else was in the building. There was no one on the line when she picked up the receiver, and she assumed she missed the call.

About to hang up, she heard, "Abigail, you there?"

It was a familiar voice, and one that she hadn't heard since Dwayne's funeral. Darnell Johnson worked for Dearborn Police. Other than being a cop, he was nothing like his brother, The Rock. She had only met him a couple times, once at a charity function with Dwayne, and at the funeral. She didn't know about the friction between the brothers or why they rarely spoke to each other.

Abigail answered cordially. "Darnell, what a nice surprise, how have you been?"

"Hey, Abigail, chasing scumbags and trying my best to lock up a few. You know how it is."

Johnson got right to it.

"That's why I'm calling...got a sexually motivated homicide that I plugged into ViCLAS. Saw that you have a case that matches the M.O... the vic took one to the balls, another to the heart. Looks like he bled out before the second shot."

Brown eyed the blueberry muffin she planned on having with her morning tea.

"That sounds like the one I had about a month ago, but it went cold as fast as the Lions."

Johnson forced a chuckle.

"Figures, thought I'd check anyway. I know how short-handed you guys are, but was hoping there might be follow-up that hadn't made it to the file."

Abigail powered up her laptop.

"I'd like to give you more than what you've got now, but I'm not on the case anymore."

"The file has you listed as lead investigator."

"What can I say, office politics. I'm not too popular around here since...you know, when your brother..."

"That's bullshit. I hope you know that I don't blame you for Dwayne's death. He knew the risk when he put on the badge."

"Thanks, I appreciate the vote of confidence. Did you try calling one of the other Detectives? They might have more for you."

"You mean Ding and Dong? I met those idiots at the funeral. They were so far up your Captain's ass...don't get me going about Captain Cracker. Pretended like he was Dwayne's favorite white uncle. Dumbass didn't even spell his name right on the memorial plaque they gave me."

Abigail unlocked her desk drawers.

"Guess you know what I'm dealing with here."

"My bad. Sorry to dump on you so early in the morning, but Dwayne told me once how you like to get an early start."

"I thought you two didn't talk much?"

"We didn't—story for another day. He really liked you, couldn't say enough after they teamed you up. Anyway, I gotta go...been working this case all night. Let me know if you hear anything else?"

"You bet. Nice talking to you."

She hung up the phone and brought up the Molina case on her computer. There'd been no supplementary reports added to the file. If there was any new information, she knew no one would tell her about it. Abigail spooned her tea bag inside the cup and stared at the lifeless art on her wall. She wondered if there was anything she could do on the Molina case.

While she recalled the poor bastard with his balls blown off, Alice Campbell popped into her head. One thing had nothing to do with the other, but her left brain was competing with her right brain for attention. Like a jack-in-the-box she popped up from her chair and headed for the Gang Squad's office on the second floor.

She caught Alice coming in the door, juggling her gloves, Starbucks coffee, purse, and key card. Abigail grabbed the door before her old friend dropped something.

"Thanks. Where've you been hiding? Haven't seen much of you since you came back from..."

"I know, I know, been meaning to stop by and say hey, but the Captain's been dumping files on me like I'm a recycling depot. He expects me to miraculously solve all the freaking cases that sat in a pile on my desk while I was gone."

"I hear you, girl, it's no different around here, just a different asshole for a boss. Mine spends more time staring at my tits than he does reading files."

They both laughed. Alice dumped everything but the coffee on top of a file cabinet and pointed to a chair for Abigail. The two women went through the police academy together, but worked in different areas and followed different career paths. Campbell sat down behind her desk, popped the lid off her coffee and took a sip.

"What brings you all the way down to the second floor?"

"You heard of the knock-out game, or anything like that where bangers are randomly clocking people on the street, trying to put their lights out?"

Alice took another sip of coffee and nodded.

"Yeah, one of my CI's said he did one. His initiation. I got the impression it was an isolated incident. He said they had to commit a criminal offence and have one of the other members witness it. I'm sorry, but I didn't give it much thought at the time. He didn't know his victim and I had no reason to follow up on it."

"Don't fret. Nobody knows shit about it. I got the scoop from a cop in New York. They've had a big problem with it there. Some bangers turned it into a game where they get points and keep fucking score."

Alice smirked. Abigail gave her a sideways glance. They were the same age, but her white friend's grey roots in her blonde hair, and the web of wrinkles around her eyes and mouth added years to her appearance.

"I'm sorry. It's not funny...I miss your potty mouth. We need to go out and get shit-faced."

Abigail smiled, realized it was the first time she'd done so in a long time.

"You're right, we'll do it soon. If I send you some suspect descriptions and geography for the occurrences, can you take a look and come up with some names for me?"

A huge black cop that looked more like an offensive lineman, stuck his head in the door of Alice's office.

"LT wants to see you...seems pissed. Don't think he ate his Captain Crunch this morning."

"Thanks, Wally, I'll be right there."

She rolled her eyes.

"Duty calls. Send me what you've got and I'll try to get back to you by the end of the day, depending on what the boss has in store for me."

"You're the best. I'm gonna look at my calendar too and throw some dates at you."

Abigail left her friend's office and headed up to her own.

Ten

Marketing

Dion Davies always wanted to belong, whether it was Neighborhood Watch or a neighborhood gang. He was small, thin, and immature for his age, and always an easy mark for bullies both at school and on the block where he lived. It wasn't until he met Corey Talbot, who gave him the street name 'D', that he felt he belonged to something larger than himself.

They met at a video store, the two of them shared an interest in PlayStation and Xbox games. Dion worked at the store part time, and either passed on his employee discount or his own game rentals to his only friend. Cory invited him to join the 'Gamers', a street gang from the Brewster-Douglas Housing Projects in East Detroit.

Dion was flattered by the offer, but balked at the invitation when he found out the initiation entailed breaking the law by either assaulting someone or robbing a store. He knew his limits and lacked the courage to commit such an act. He declined the offer. Cory talked his fellow gangbangers into allowing Dion to hang with them on the condition he used his camera and video skills to record their escapades.

His mother had called him a retard and left him with his grandmother at an early age. He never knew who his father was. He didn't do well in school and had been held back more than once. Dion's grandma worked so it was easy for him to skip school and hang out with his homies.

Cory was a different story, the perfect example of a juvenile delinquent. His father was in jail for murder and his mother had died of a drug overdose. He'd been in and out of the foster system until the day he finally escaped. He flopped with friends and fellow bangers. His street name was C Dawg. His lengthy criminal record included everything from shoplifting to car theft.

The two young men waited, tucked away out of the wind in the recessed doorway of a boarded-up restaurant on Russell Street in the Eastern Market. The sun's rays offered a taste of spring, but the nip in the air meant old man winter had not packed his bags yet. C Dawg turned to D and asked if the camera was on. He needed to better another gamer called 666.

The banger eyed a shopper on a bicycle coming from the market. He carried a backpack. They scored more points for a moving target. The cyclist rode the sidewalk, unaware of what lurked in the shadows ahead of him. He held the handlebars with one hand and thumbed his phone with the other.

C Dawg lurched from the doorway and threw a roundhouse with his right hand. When his fist was mid-air, and his weight behind him, the cyclist dropped his phone, and bent down to try and grab it. The punch went over the man's head, and C's momentum threw him into his victim and the bicycle. They crashed to the sidewalk.

D watched in awe as the scene unfolded and recorded every move. When he looked up to check on his homey, he caught movement with his peripheral vision. He glanced in that direction and saw a black woman running full speed toward them.

Norm Strom had been back from his two-month South American adventure for a couple weeks, and he was on a mission to reconnect with family and friends he hadn't seen for a while. He called Bill Meyers, in Detroit, and suggested they hook up for lunch. It would be a perfect chance to check up on his buddy's niece, Miss Brown.

The world traveler liked to tell people that he wasn't a wine connoisseur, just a sewer. In reality, he'd taken the first year of a master taster's course, and further educated himself in Argentina and Chile, learning about Malbec and Carmenere. While in Detroit, Norm thought he'd stop in at his favorite wine store in the Eastern Market.

After crossing the border and checking in with the owner of the shop, they chatted about the wines he'd sampled south of the equator. The proprietor looked more like a beer drinker, with a gut bigger than Norm's. He had a room in the back where he'd invite his preferred customers for tastings. The two men sampled a few vintages.

Norm was disappointed in the lack of South American wines, especially Malbec from the Mendoza region, where he'd fell in love with the grape that was so popular there. He left the store with a case of assorted bottles from Spain, Australia, and California.

He drove north on Russell Street. While eyeing the meat market across the street, a black woman appeared directly in front of him on the road. Running full tilt, she chased two young black men in hoodies. Nearby a white man lay on the sidewalk holding one knee, as if in severe pain.

Norm was retired and had been out of the game for a few years, but it was obvious to him that something bad happened, and that the woman, possibly a cop, chased those men for a reason. He braked hard to avoid hitting the woman, and glanced to his left to see where they went. It was all a blur, but he thought the woman looked familiar.

Detective Brown received a list of suspects as promised by her friend, Alice. She spent hours going over their rap sheets, checking the victim's descriptions for possible matches, and mapping various locations of the assaults. She pinpointed two separate areas where gang activity had been reported, the heaviest being around the Eastern Market, near the Brewster-Douglas Projects. That's where she'd start.

Abigail didn't bother to ask for help with surveillance in the targeted area, she knew what the answer would be. It wasn't a big deal; she was used to flying solo. She knew that identifying potential targets in broad daylight would be easier than at night, but it would be a challenge to blend in and not get burned.

She waited until after lunch since that's when the occurrences took place. The Detective knew from experience, dirt bags seldom got out of bed before noon. She grabbed plastic shopping bags and a few boxes from one of the market stores to use as props. Abigail parked her car on the street or in lots, where she had a clear view of the surrounding area. The first two locations she tried were a bust.

The third spot looked promising. She'd found a spot to park on Russell Street, and popped the trunk to give the appearance she was loading groceries. Within minutes, two black males walked by her and ducked into a doorway. Like the suspects she sought, they wore dark clothes and hoodies, but so did every other banger in the area.

A man on a bicycle pedalled past her. He was wearing a backpack and doing something on his cell phone. When he rode past the doorway one of the suspects jumped out and swung at him. He missed and they crashed onto the sidewalk. Brown was into a full sprint before they stopped rolling around. The smaller suspect spotted her, grabbed his accomplice by the arm, and they ran across the street.

Eleven

The Detroit Shuffle

In his cop days, Norm Strom could have been the one in a foot chase. He had a few over the years. Seeing how fast the two suspects moved, he knew he couldn't have caught them on his best day. It was something he let the anxious young rookies do when the situation arose. He saw the trio disappear behind the meat store. The female cop was fast too. Could it really be her?

Not wanting to get involved, but curious to see if the woman was who he hoped it might be, Norm drove around the block. He caught a glimpse of them crossing the alley and heading east behind a row of warehouses. The woman hadn't gained on the two men, but she wasn't too far behind them.

The retired Detective turned on Erskine and saw them run into a park. The two men split up; the woman followed the taller one west through the playground. The shorter man lagged behind. Norm saw him slow his pace, and continue southwest towards a street on the opposite side of the green space.

He drove to Chrysler Drive, where the suspect had slowed to a fast walk. Norm rolled down his window to get a better look. He heard a female voice in the distance yelling, "Stop, Police!"

It had to be Abigail Brown. What could he do to help? He reached under the seat and grabbed his old night stick. It was there just in case, but hadn't seen any action in many years.

The suspect's head swivelled, checking for the heat. He barely gave Norm's vehicle a glance. Strom timed it perfectly and blocked the young man's path as he was about to cross the street. He may have thought about running, but he was panting and breathing so hard it appeared he had nothing left to give.

Norm jumped out of his car and flashed his badge. It read 'Retired Detective', but there was no chance the punk had time to see that. His eyes were on the circular black object in the big white man's hand. It could have been a gun barrel. Instinctively, the kid's hands shot into the air above his head. Norm went with it.

"Don't move. You're under arrest. Turn around and put your hands behind your back."

He grabbed his hoodie and pulled it down over his arms, forcing them to stay behind his back. Norm opened the back door on the passenger side of his Chevy Impala. It could have been an undercover police car for all the kid knew. The retired cop realized he'd forgotten to frisk the suspect. Not smart, it'd been a while.

He felt a bulge inside the front of the young man's waistband, the shape wasn't right for a gun. Relieved, Norm removed a camcorder and tossed it into the car. He buckled the suspect in and pulled the belt tight to keep his arms pinned behind him.

Horns honked and tires screeched on the Chrysler Freeway. Norm looked across the Interstate and saw the other suspect do a front flip over the chain-link fence on the opposite side. It slowed the cop down. She appeared to get hung up on the top for a few seconds.

Being familiar with the area, Norm drove to Mack Avenue, knowing it would take him across the highway. By the time he got over to the western side there was no sign of either the suspect or the police officer. If it was Abigail Brown, he hoped she was okay.

When he wasn't scouring the neighborhood, Norm checked the kid in his back seat. He craned his neck and snapped his head back and forth, trying to spot his friend. Norm asked where he might be, but the kid remained tight-lipped.

While cruising along the curb on Mack Avenue, he saw his favorite hot chocolate. She came from behind a housing project. Her eyes locked on Norm's car. She squinted and tilted her head as if thinking about something. She smiled and nodded slowly. He stopped as she approached.

"Norm Strom, what the hell are you doing here?"

"Helping you catch bad guys."

Probably because of the tinted windows, she didn't notice the kid in the back seat. Norm checked her out from head to toe and remembered how nice the package was.

"I almost had him...fast fucker. Lost him in the projects. Should have went after the other one, he was slower."

"You need a lift back to your car, officer?"

The smile was still there and she appeared happy to see him. Abigail walked around to the passenger side and opened the door.

"What the..."

"Found this kid walking to the projects after you wore him out. Was an easy catch.

Detective Brown got in the car, gave the suspect a glare that almost scared Norm. The smile was gone, but when she turned back to Norm, her eyes said she was glad he was there.

"My white knight...you're too much. Can you take me back to my car? I have to call this in and see if the victim is still around."

They drove back to the Eastern Market, eyeballed and smiled at each other, unsure of what to say. It had been a while, they had lots to catch up on. Abigail pointed to her car and Norm stopped behind it on Russell Street. The victim was long gone. She grabbed the kid and removed him from the back seat. Surprised when his arm came loose, she glanced back at Norm.

"Aren't you resourceful...a Canadian cop trick or something you saw on MacGyver?"

"Wait till you see my gun and badge."

She shook her head in disbelief.
"Know where the new station is?"
"Yes, officer."
"Meet me there. We need to talk."

Twelve

Home Movies

In all the excitement, Norm forgot he was supposed to meet Bill Meyers for lunch. When he called to apologize and explained how he almost literally ran into Abigail, her uncle graciously forgave him. Norm asked for a rain check, said he had to supply the police with a statement as to his involvement. Myers was curious, Strom said it was a story for another day.

The new police headquarters was a modern marvel compared to its predecessor. Norm was surprised by the lack of activity at the front desk. It was manned by two private security guards. One of them asked his business there, and the other called Detective Brown's extension. There was no response. He took a seat while they tried the direct line for Major Crimes.

Norm studied the boring architecture in the main lobby for something to do. His eyelids grew heavy. The alcohol from wine sampling on an empty stomach, made him drowsy. After a couple of head bobs, he picked up the suspect's video camera from the seat beside him and turned it on.

He played with the buttons and was able to rewind the video that appeared on the viewing screen. The taller of the two suspects was captured in action, attempting to throw a punch at a cyclist on the sidewalk near the Eastern Market. Norm deduced the perp he captured did the filming.

The video showed a collision between the suspect and cyclist, a quick glimpse of Abigail running in their direction, and jumbled images of feet and pavement while the street punks ran from the scene. The camera remained on during the foot chase. At the park, when the two split up, the image came back into focus showing the Detective pursuing the taller suspect across the freeway.

Norm continued to rewind the video and saw more footage of people and places he didn't recognize. There was evidence of another assault, the idiots kept a record of their crimes. He continued watching the video to stay awake.

One of the security guards called his name and waved him towards the desk. Norm followed him to the Detective office. The retired Windsor cop was surprised at how roomy, but sparse the interior of the building was. The old HQ had been packed wall to wall with desks and file cabinets.

Security led Norm to an office on the third floor. Abigail sat behind her desk, talking on the phone. His friend held up a finger to signal she'd be a minute and pointed to the empty chair between her and the door.

He scanned her office. It was more than the cubicle he'd had when he worked for a living, and hers had a door, but the glass walls didn't rise to the ceiling.

Norm was perusing the collage on her wall when Abigail hung up the phone.

"What's that you're holding?"

"Camcorder. Forgot about it after I saw you...took it off the punk I nabbed. Should be a slam-dunk case. The morons videotaped everything they did."

"You're shitting me."

"I shit you not, Detective."

She leaned forward, held out her hands.

"Can I see the playback on here? Don't think it can be hooked up to my lap top."

Norm handed her the video recorder, showed her which buttons to push.

"You can watch it in reverse, or go back further and hit play."

Abigail played with the buttons, watched the film, and shook her head.

"That's what I was afraid of. The punch he threw never connected with the victim. As of now, we don't know exactly who he was. I was just on the phone with the ADA."

She glanced up at Norm.

"That's *Assistant District Attorney* on our side of the border. He's checking for precedent to see if we can lay an assault charge."

Norm nodded.

"We call them *Crown Attorneys*. Wouldn't the collision constitute an assault, whether or not the punch landed? Although I do understand how you'd need a victim...or some complainant."

Abigail moved her head up and down, her eyes on the video.

"You're right, these bangers really are morons. I definitely see some other assaults on here. I need to watch some more of this before I interview your guy. You want something to eat or drink?"

"Yes. Maybe what you call soda and candy bar, here in America. I was supposed to have lunch with your Uncle Bill, but then I ran into you."

"I'm sorry about lunch. There are vending machines in the hall, where you came in."

Norm smiled, got up.

"Okay. I'm starving, you watch the video and I'm going for junk food. Want anything?"

She didn't take her eyes off the viewfinder and waved him off. Norm took a walk. There were two other Detectives in the office across from Abigail's. They eyeballed him like he'd just pulled off a prison escape. He offered a polite nod and went for food.

Thirteen

Blessed Art Thou

Norm selected a Kit Kat Chunky and a Diet Coke from the machines in the third-floor hallway. There was nothing healthy. He reached the door at Major Crimes at the same time as a well-dressed black officer about his age.

With a mouth full of chocolate, Norm held the door open and waved the man in ahead of him. The man gave him a quick scan from head to toe, probably looking for the guest pass he'd left with his coat in Abigale's office.

As Norm stepped aside to follow him in the door, the man nodded and said, "Thank you, sir, and God bless you."

The retired Windsor cop nodded back, then continued across the room to his friend's office. The other two Dicks he'd seen were still chatting, but made it obvious they were aware of him. Norm nodded politely again, then returned to Abigail's office. She was busy flipping through pictures on her phone.

"Keep any pics of me on there?"

She smiled.

"We can catch up later, Norman, I'm trying to find...holy shit!"

He thought about it for a second, only his mother had ever called him that.

"What've you got?"

She stared at the phone another few seconds, and glanced across the hall at the other two Dicks.

"You work with those guys? They sure checked me out."

"Tintenelli and Walker...I'll fill you in later. Shit."

"That's two shits, one of them holy. What's up?"

Abigail got up and closed her door. Norm glanced up, wondered what difference it made with the open space above the wall. She handed him her phone.

He checked the displayed photo. She grabbed the camcorder off her desk and handed it to him. Norm looked at both devices, the video was paused on an image that appeared to be the same as the one on her phone. Norm held them side by side for comparison.

"Cool. Same house...someone you know?"

Abigail hushed her voice, put Norm between her and the prying eyes across the hall as if they were listening.

"It's a murder house. Guy got his balls blown off before he got finished off with another shot to the chest. It was my case until the two clowns behind you took it over and called it a serial. Too bad for them, it's a cold case now."

Norm handed her the camera and phone, grinned, and raised his eyebrows.

"Cold until now. Tell me.... what do you think?"

She returned to her desk, tapped on her computer's keyboard.

"I need to look through my files on the murder. I doubt the two bangers had anything to do with whacking the guy, but I'd be interested in knowing when they were there. That car wasn't there when I was...maybe they know something about it...or the house. Why did they film the house?

It was dark and they were in the car...looks like a Chrysler 300...maybe they tried to boost it. There are shadows near the house. Looks like the tall banger was near the windows checking things out. I have to get this to our tech people to make a better copy."

Norm pursed his lips.

"Sounds like a solid lead, you gonna question the banger I grabbed?"

"For sure... sweating him in an interview room right now. I was just about to visit him..."

Someone knocked on the door, then stepped in. It was the well-dressed Detective Norm ran into earlier.

"Sorry to interrupt, Abigail, do you have someone in custody I should know about?"

"Yes, Lieutenant, a young banger I'm holding for an assault near the Eastern Market. I think he's one of a pair working the area and playing the Knock-out game."

He shifted to face Norm.

"Oh, my bad, LT. This is retired Police Detective Norm Strom, from Canada. He witnessed the assault and made a citizen's arrest on one of the gang bangers. He retrieved a video recorder from the kid...he'd taped the whole thing."

Her boss offered his hand.

"Lieutenant Robinson, Detective Strom, nice to make your acquaintance. Very commendable of you...aiding of one our own like that. You happened to be in the area?"

"I'd just left the wine store in the Eastern Market, and was going to meet one of your retired officers...an old friend of mine. Once a cop, always a cop. It was the least I could do."

He stepped back towards the door.

"God bless you. I'll let you get back to it, Abigail, make sure you leave me a copy of your report. I'm heading out early...have a doctor's appointment."

"Hope it's nothing serious, LT."

He turned to leave.

"Routine checkup. God bless you both."

Robinson closed the door on the way out of her office.

Norm gawked at Abigail, offered a toothy smile.

"What? She asked.

"Just basking in the glow...he blessed me three times, I feel like I need to go to church."

Abigail chuckled.

"Robinson would like that...religious is a good word to describe him."

She slouched in her chair, gazed at Norm. He remembered the look from their night out to dinner at Niagara-on-the-Lake. Her eyes the color of chestnuts, it was as if they could see into his soul. There in her office, he got that feeling in his gut again. He was fresh clay in her hands. He wondered if she knew how easily she could mould him into her masterpiece.

"What's next ...you want me to write out a statement?"

She held her gaze on him a few more seconds, leaned forward, and put her business face back on.

"Yes. How bout I give you my laptop...I'll bring up a blank statement form. Then I'm going to question are little gang banger."

"I don't mean to tell you how to do your job, Abigail, but you know he's not going to give up his buddy on the assaults."

"I've got them on tape...all I need is his name. You have some advice for me?"

"I used to be pretty good in the room, in my day. But this is your case. Tell him straight up you witnessed the assault and he's going down for it. That should get him to lawyer up."

She scrunched her face.

"And how does that help me?"

"You leave the room for a few minutes and tell him you've called him a lawyer...that it will take a while, and he doesn't have to say anything. Then you tell him a story about a murder and how you've seen the video and he's going to jail for the rest of his life...that the car they were in was stolen and his prints will match. It'll give him lots of things to think about.

Remind him he doesn't have to say anything about the assault charge, but he can help himself and his friend if he tells you about the murder house, and what they did there. Maybe throw in something about them matching a witness' description of them at the scene.

He should have forgotten about the assault by that time and be crying about not doing any murder. Ask him to prove he and his friend weren't involved, even though they're on the video. Fish around to see if he'll offer his buddy's name to verify his story and how they were only there for the car or whatever."

"Christ, Norm, I should put you in there with him...you're a better bull-shitter than I am. You know I can't let you in the box. Maybe you can keep an eye out while writing your statement in the viewing room."

Norm shrugged.

"Works for me. Like I said, it's your case."

Fourteen

Boxed In

The retired Fraud and Arson Detective peered into the empty interview room, while setting up the laptop and positioning his chair for a ringside seat. He remembered his past interrogations; some good and some bad. There was a science to doing it well, but nothing guaranteed a positive outcome. He'd gotten some good confessions, but also been told to go fuck himself.

From years of experience, Norm learned that most criminals were stupid, especially those who'd been caught in the act. Ironically, those were the hardest to get to admit incriminating statements. He'd also discovered that most people like to talk, and that was the key. Get them to talk about anything and chances were they'd either slip up or break down and confess.

He was two paragraphs into his statement, when Abigail entered the box with the young gang banger. He seemed smaller, funny how only a few hours in custody can knock someone down a few notches. Norm continued typing while she explained the necessary legal mumbo-jumbo.

His statement had become a short story, he'd written hundreds over the years. As much as Norm liked to add a little spice or touch of comedy to his version of events, he had to remember that his work would be read by prosecutors, lawyers, and judges, most of whom had no sense of humor. So what if he liked to have a bit of fun while he worked. It's how he kept his sanity throughout his thirty-one years on the job.

Detective Brown got into collecting the tombstone information, confirming things like his full name, date of birth, and address for the record. Norm took pause, surveyed Abigail's layout of the room, as well as the demeanor of both her and the accused. She oozed professionalism. Sat perfectly straight, spoke clear and concise—not always attributes that helped when dealing with a street punk who held a single digit IQ.

It was as if she'd received Norm's thoughts telepathically, and suddenly realized who she was talking to. The Major Crimes Detective got up from her chair and took her jacket off. She asked Dion if he wanted something to drink. He shook his head. He took in the room and held his gaze on the mirrored glass for a moment. Probably wondering who was behind it.

Abigail asked questions about family, school, and friends, but his answers were either nods or head shakes. The good news what that he had not yet asked for a lawyer. Norm kept an ear open while he went back to typing his story. She asked him about sports and games.

Norm caught movement in the corner of his eye. Dion had adjusted himself in his seat. The Detective saw that she was on the right track and started naming video games that she was aware of. He'd been gazing down, head buried. It popped up like he'd just pulled it from the sand. The corners of his mouth formed a smile. Knowing she was headed in the right direction, Abigail asked what games he liked.

Finally, the kid spoke. Norm had no idea what he was talking about, and it was probably the same for her, but she nodded in acknowledgement and let him talk. While he explained his skill level in the gaming world, Abigail removed his phone from an evidence bag and asked him to show her his favorite games.

The door behind Norm opened and one of the Detectives who'd been eyeballing him earlier stepped into the room. With his peripheral vision, the retired Canadian Cop continued typing and pretended to ignore him. The suit cleared his throat a couple times, making his presence known, but Norm kept his eyes on the laptop screen and ears on the conversation on the other side of the glass.

Dion pointed out a few screen icons and she scrolled through them as though she was interested. She asked him about the knock-out game. He broke eye contact with her and didn't answer. Committed, she removed his camcorder from another evidence bag and put in on the table between them. The kid fidgeted in his seat.

Realizing she was taking a chance, and that she might have lost him, Abigail queued up the video to the murder house. She handed the camcorder to Dion and asked him to hit play. He watched in silence, raised an eyebrow as though he'd forgotten that portion of the tape.

He handed the recorder back to the Detective and shrugged. Detective Brown laid out her sales pitch. She said it was obvious from the video that they were playing the knock-out game, but it was the house on Charlevoix that she was more concerned about. It was the scene of a murder at the same time and date of his recording. The big cop behind Norm grunted and left the room.

It was as if she'd poked Dion with a sharp stick. He jumped back in his seat, shook his head violently, and repeated the word 'no' about a dozen times. He said they had nothing to do with it...that they were going to boost the car but got scared off. The kid pressed his lips together as if to stop himself from saying anything more. Abigail went at him again, throwing words like witnesses and forensics at him.

Norm stopped typing. The action in the box was entertaining. Abigail's interrogation style impressed him. She'd taken some of his advice and put her own spin on it. The kid was on the edge of his seat...he wanted to talk...you could almost see the words forming in his brain.

Instead of asking him directly who his accomplice was, Abigail told him she already had an idea. She would show the witness their photos, and prints found on the window of the house would no doubt match one of them. Dion's had been taken earlier and were being compared as they spoke.

The young man trembled as if he was about to cry. He told her again that they were only interested in the car and what was in it. They'd seen a briefcase on the seat. He slipped. Dion said Corey wanted to make sure nobody could see out the windows in the house. Abigail didn't interrupt. They heard what sounded like a gunshot, and ran off.

He said that was it...nothing to do with any murder...that they left the car and the area. He told her to check the video again. It proved they never went into the house or the car. Detective Brown interrupted and asked for Corey's last name. Dion hesitated. Abigail said she would need to talk to his friend to confirm their story that they had nothing to do with the murder. Dion thought about it and remained tight-lipped.

She asked if he remembered anything else. Did he hear more than one gunshot? He shook his head and said one was enough to make them run. The Detective asked him to describe the car and anything they saw inside it. He mentioned doctor's headphones hanging on the rear-view mirror. He thought they were cool. What he meant was a stethoscope, but he lacked the vocabulary.

Dion drew her a picture of a parking permit he'd seen on the windshield. He slid the piece of paper across the desk to Abigail. He told her his homey's name was Corey Talbot...he went by C Dawg on the street...and he wasn't a bad kid. For him, it was all about games. Abigail took another shot and asked about the Knock-out game. Dion shook his head and looked away.

Someone knocked on the interrogation room door. It must have been something important. Norm knew from experience you didn't interrupt unless it was urgent. Abigail got up and responded. It was the big cop that had walked in on him. He looked more Mafioso than Detective, with his slicked back hair and expensive suit. He and Brown had a brief conversation in the doorway.

She told Dion to sit tight. She packed up her notes and the evidence bags. Abigail stepped into Norm's room. Her sad eyes and demeanor gave him the impression that someone she knew had just died. He gave her a 'what's up' nod.

"Tintenelli says the Captain wants to see me."

She shook her head.

"They know about the kid in the other room, and my new lead that ties him to the murder."

"He was in here. He listened in on your conversation with Dion."

"What! Which part?"

"He wasn't in here long, but his timing was perfect. It was when you brought up the time stamp on the video at the murder house."

"Shit! I'm fucked. Tintenelli and Walker are lead on that case, and are no doubt in the boss' office right now, crying about me poaching their case."

Norm picked up the laptop, stood in front of Abigail and placed a hand on her shoulder.

"This crap reminds me why I don't miss the job."

Fifteen

Office Politics

Norm didn't bother to ask what was going on, he'd dealt with prima donnas in major crimes on his side of the border. At Abigail's suggestion, he set up shop in her office to finish his statement. The report was basically complete. He only needed to proofread it and check for typos. Detective Brown's aquarium was the perfect place to keep an eye on the action across the room.

He didn't need to hear the words. The actions and gestures spoke volumes. The three were in the Captain's office. He was shouldered by the two male Dicks. They looked like offensive linemen protecting their quarterback. They were all over Abigail, alone on defense.

The shouting and finger pointing went on for about five minutes. When she returned to her office, she looked like a dog who'd been scolded for peeing on the carpet. With her tail between her legs, and eyes that revealed anger more than sorrow, she grabbed her purse and coat.

"Leave that shit. Let's get the fuck outa here."

At his suggestion, he took her to a bar on Monroe, where he hoped there'd be no other cops. He'd been there years earlier with some Ontario Provincial Police undercover operators. They worked a sting operation together. The guys liked the bartender. She bared her tits for tips.

They sat in a dark corner with their backs to the wall. Even in retirement, it was habitual for Norm. He ordered a pint of an Irish Red. She ordered a glass of cab. It was obvious to him that

Abigail was upset when she didn't ask what vintages were available.

She sipped her wine, stared into the space above and beyond Norm's head. He let her be, scanned the room, and marvelled at the antique wooden bar. He thought it might be carved black walnut. Pillars rose from the counter to the ceiling. Behind it mirrors reflected and doubled a colourful selection of booze bottles.

His eyes came to rest on Abigail. She was one of the most beautiful women he'd ever experienced. In heels, she nearly matched his seventy-three inches height. Dark chocolate eyes with milk chocolate skin...she was curvaceous, but slim. He removed her clothes in his mind, and remembered the only time they had sex.

"What are smiling at, mister?"

He was busted. She knew exactly what he was thinking.

"Sweet memories...something to cheer you up. It's only work. There's a lot more to life. Believe me, I'm living proof."

"You surely are...South America huh? Do tell. Hook up with any Brazilian babes?"

Norm finished his beer, held up the empty glass for the waitress to see, and signalled her for another round.

"I didn't get to Brazil, wasn't in the plan. Peru, Chile, and Argentina. You would have loved Machu Picchu...and Mendoza...the wine region. I have to admit I fell in love with a woman there named Malbec."

Abigail smiled.

"Cheers to you. You always know how to make me smile. I read your emails. Tell me about that lake with the floating grass islands. It had a dirty name."

Norm chuckled.

"Lake Titicaca...the indigenous people build their huts and boats and islands from reeds that are lashed together."

She put her elbows on the table and leaned in. He told her how the natives lived, and how they had to anchor their islands so the wind didn't blow them across the lake. He went on about his mountain trek to sacred Inca villages, and the wine tour in the mountains of Argentina.

They laughed about Norm's adventures and misadventures. He switched to wine and ordered a bottle of Chilean Cabernet Sauvignon. They nibbled on an appetizer platter and talked about exotic places on their bucket lists. When the trip they'd taken to Niagara came up, Abigail looked at her watch.

"We need to talk about that, my friend, but not tonight. Work has me frustrated and worn out, and I have to get back at it tomorrow. Maybe I can do some damage control with...never mind, I don't want to bring myself down again. It was great having you almost run into me today. Can you drop me off at home?"

Norm signalled the waitress for the check.

"You still living in the same place, downtown?"

Abigail nodded, got up and put on her coat.

They didn't speak in the car, she stared out the window while Norm drove. It was less than a mile to her place. He stopped out front and waited for her to look at him. She hesitated for a moment. Abigail turned, smiled, and then kissed him on the cheek. On the way out of the car she spoke over her shoulder.

"Thanks, Norman. I'll call you tomorrow."

Sixteen

Dreams & Nightmares

Abigail dropped her purse and coat as she walked through the door. She peeled and kicked each boot off, and stumbled into the living room. For a second, she considered another glass of wine, but didn't feel like cracking a bottle. She was too dead tired. The physical aspect of her life and being on her feet all day posed no problem for her. It was the mental game that wore her down.

Brown powered up the laptop, then continued to shed clothes on the way to her bedroom. The apartment was usually neat, but she let her clothes lay where they fell. Donning a tee shirt and sweats, she sat down behind the computer. There was only one email, it was from her Uncle Bill. He wanted to know how it went with Norm.

With Dion's sketch fresh in her mind, Abigail googled local hospitals and checked their logos. She thought the stethoscope belonged to a medical professional who paid for permit parking at their place of employment.

She woke up staring at the web page for an animal hospital. Dazed and confused, Abigail realized she'd nodded off. The time stamp on the screen said it had only been minutes, but it seemed longer. She dreamt a replay of her foot chase across the Interstate. In the imaginary version, C Dawg got hit by a truck. Her head felt like it was filled with warm water. She closed the laptop and headed for bed.

Norm crossed the border into Canada, and headed for home. He took the scenic route and drove east on Riverside Drive. It offered an amazing view of Detroit during the day or night. He gazed across the river and thought about the first time he'd met

Abigail Brown. It was at a Tigers ball game, while he visited Bill Meyers.

They watched the game from a vacant executive box. The retired Detroit cop played dumb when a beautiful black woman stepped in and sat down between them. She said hello to Norm, and offered him a big smile. It made him wonder if he knew her. Had he met her before? Meyers had prepped her beforehand.

He and his niece carried on the charade for a few minutes. He shrugged as if he was clueless, when Norm looked at him to see what was going on. Embarrassed, Norm blushed when she asked why he didn't remember her. He searched his memory in vain, but had no idea who the attractive woman was. She leaned in to kiss him on the cheek. Bill couldn't contain himself and laughed out loud.

When the woman joined in, Norm knew he'd been had. His American friend apologized and introduced his niece, Abigail Brown. Being a good sport, Norm laughed along with them.

When Meyers got a call to attend his office, ebony and ivory remained in their seats. They talked about everything except the ball game. The Tigers were losing anyway. There was a comfort level they both enjoyed. It was as if they'd known each other for years.

Abigail recently ended a relationship and Norm was seeing someone regularly. They spoke openly about the passion and pitfalls of dating, and shared their humorous and horror stories. Norm was surprised, but glad, when she suggested he let her know the next time he hooked up with her Uncle.

* * *

Dion Davies had never been to jail, but he'd heard all about it from his homies. They joked around and told him if he ever went in, he'd become someone's bitch in no time. Detective

Brown told him he'd only be in overnight. He'd be arraigned in the morning and then released sometime after that. She said she'd talk to him then.

He was placed in a holding cell with mostly other men of the same color. There was no room to sit so he stood. Being fresh meat on the block, he felt like a chicken leg at a family barbeque. Dion was terrified. He was living a nightmare. He folded his arms across his chest to stop himself from shaking.

The young wannabe banger tried to avoid one particular set of eyes. They were fixed on him. He was determined not to turn his back on that guy. Dion never saw who grabbed him from behind. A strong arm applied a choke hold.

His vision blurred. There was no air in his lungs. He clawed at the forearm and kicked at the shins of his attacker. His energy waned. He saw his mother standing in the kitchen, stirring a pot of soup on the stove. She turned to wave. Her warm smile was the last thing Dion Davies ever saw.

Seventeen

A New Day

It was a new day. Abigail awoke before her alarm. She sprung from bed as if it were on fire, pulled back the curtain, and peered out the window. No snow. After a quick pit stop in the bathroom, she took to the living room floor to stretch. Her brain on autopilot, she downed a glass of water, laced her shoes, and bundled up for her morning run.

It was quiet and dark as usual, but unseasonably mild. A warm front had crept up from the south overnight, the sidewalk and road were damp from rain instead of covered in snow. She headed in the opposite direction of her usual route; it was time to change things up.

Maybe that's what her life needed, change. Norm Strom came to mind. It wasn't the first time she'd considered stepping it up a notch with him. Was she ready to commit to a new relationship? Was he the one? Did he feel the same way? She'd asked herself those questions before, but never really answered them. Was she afraid to start over and maybe get hurt again?

She tripped over uneven sidewalk and made a mental note to watch the ground for such impediments. The damp air weighed heavy in her lungs; its warmth didn't sting like the recent bitterness.

A man from the Detroit News filled the newspaper box on a street corner. He stared. She wondered if he was surprised to see someone else on the street at that time of the morning, or if he was a pervert checking her out. Her job made it hard not to think that way.

Abigail thought about her workday and how she would press Dion to get Corey and more information about the Molina murder. Walker and Tintenelli wouldn't be happy about her sticking her nose in their case. Too bad...she's the one who came up with the lead. She'd have to be careful how she went about it and keep her distance from the Captain.

Detective Brown got to work early, as usual. She almost dropped her coffee when she saw the dynamic duo hunched over the desk in their office. Tintenelli's suit jacket hung on the back of his chair, soiled and one elbow torn. His normally neat and slicked back hair resembled a bad wig.

Walker looked like he'd gotten into a pickup game of football with his old friends. His shirt was torn at the collar, and he wore a Band-Aid over his left eyebrow. The purple ring below it was a shiner in the making.

Trying not to be obvious about noticing them, Abigail made a beeline for her office. She didn't see Lieutenant Robinson until he called her name. She wheeled right, and stopped outside his door. He waved her in.

"Thought I'd better fill you in. Walker and Tintenelli pulled an all-nighter, and I got called in for an officer involved fatality."

In response, Brown slinked into the empty chair in front of the Lieutenant's desk.

"They followed up on that lead you gave them on their file, the Molina homicide. They ran into a bit of trouble."

"What are you talking about, I didn't give them any leads."

"I know, I know, Abigail...they said you questioned one of their witnesses. They took it from there and hunted down Corey Talbot. It got ugly."

She straightened in her chair, felt her blood getting warmer. Brown bit her lip, knowing she'd already lost the battle.

"They got into a tussle with Talbot's gang, the YBN (Young Brewster Niggas) in the projects...seems they knew the cops were coming and they weren't giving up their homey without a fight.

YBN attacked and assaulted your fellow Detectives, but they still managed to get the suspect out of the building. Unfortunately, they were jumped again by more YBN before they got to their car or backup arrived.

Talbot ran to the freeway and tried to jump from the overpass to the road below. Walker says the gang member fell into the path of a northbound truck and was run over. He died at the scene; God bless his wretched soul."

Instinctively, Abigail glanced over at the Detective. It was as if Walker knew what she was thinking, he returned the stare. His eyes revealed no shame or remorse, only an intense scowl with a hint of guilt.

"That's crazy, LT, the kid didn't do anything wrong, he was a fucking witness for god's sake."

"He wasn't an innocent. According to your own report, he was suspect in several assaults. And you know how I feel about vulgarity and using the lord's name in vain. They were only..."

Agitated, she cut him off.

"I know how they work. It's a good thing I processed Davies, at least in custody they couldn't get him killed."

Robinson dropped his eyes to the desk blotter.

"About young Dion Davies..."

"Now what? What did they do to him?"

"Detective's Walker and Tintenelli didn't do anything to him. He uh...he was murdered in the holding tank."

"What?! Are you fucking kidding me?"

The Lieutenant folded his hands in front of him. He leaned over the desk as if he was about to go into one of his sermons on life.

"Abigail, I won't respond if you continue to talk like that. Mr. Davies was attacked by an unknown assailant and choked to death. Your fellow Detectives think the word got back to the YBN that he gave up Talbot. It is unfortunate."

She threw her head back and looked to the ceiling, searched for the right words.

"Gee, I wonder how that happened. What about the cameras...that cell is under surveillance, isn't it?"

"It's supposed to be. It was in need of repairs, but you know how the bankruptcy and lack of funds has affected the budget for things like that."

"Yeah, things like preventing a murder in police custody. Unbelievable. We're supposed to protect people, not get them killed—two in one night. That's fucking insane."

Abigail sprung from her seat before the Lieutenant launched into another tirade about her language or the attributes of his saviour. She turned to leave his office and saw Tintenelli staring at her. Brown glared back at him and he flipper her the bird. It was a new day.

Eighteen

Flying Solo

Detective Brown sat quietly behind her desk and sipped her coffee. She gazed at the collage of human tragedy on the wall. All those victims and there would be no justice for them unless they considered death fair retribution.

Abigail shook her head in disbelief, *such a waste*. Talbot and Davies may have been legitimate suspects for the string of assaults, but they were also the only two potential witnesses she had for the Molina homicide.

She grabbed her breakfast muffin and put it in a desk drawer. She had no appetite. It was time to get back to work. Abigail was left to work on her own so that's exactly what she did. The assault files were closed and written off to the dead gang bangers. The Captain would be thrilled with the increase in his clearance rate.

While she browsed individual cases on her computer, the wheels turned in her head, conjuring up a plan to dig deeper into the murder investigation. Walker and Tintenelli would be hip deep in paperwork, and under the Internal Affairs microscope for a while. Their immediate concern would be covering their own asses.

She had room to fly under the radar without their interference. It took Abigail most of the morning to clear all her cases in the knock-out file. Her muffin had disappeared in the flurry of paperwork, only the few wayward crumbs that survived remained on her desk as evidence of its existence.

The caffeine boost from her second cup of coffee had the Detective raring to go. She scoured various websites, searching for logos from medical centers. It was only a hunch, but she had to start somewhere.

Her fingers worked the keyboard, eyes scanned websites, and the memory section of her brain considered the serial aspect of the crime. No matter what Walker and Tintenelli thought about their sexually motivated stabbing, she knew the two cases weren't connected.

She remembered the call from Dwayne's brother, in Dearborn, then switched screens and checked ViCLAS (Violent Crime Linkage Analysis System) looking for similar M.O.'s.

She read through Darnell's case. There were no other similar cases in the Metro-Detroit area so she expanded the search parameters. Bingo. She found one in Port Huron and another in Lansing. Abigail scratched her head as she read the files. The locations were so far apart. What was the connection?

Hungry, but too deep into the investigation to go out for lunch, Brown grabbed a quick fix from the vending machines. It meant an extra mile on the next run. She flipped through the contacts on her phone, selected Darnell Johnson's personal number, and pressed the dial button. He answered on the first ring.

"Abigail? Everything alright?"

She forced a laugh.

"I wasn't sure if you were working, so I called this number."

"No problem...yeah, I'm working...spending more time here than at home, you know how it is."

"I hear you. Too bad we don't get paid for the extra hours. Is money as tight with your department?"

"Not as bad as what I hear about your place. We have to jump through a few hoops and get permission, but we manage a little extra cash...not enough to put in the bank, mind you. So what's up?"

"You remember the double-tap killer you called me about? One in the crotch and one in the chest?"

"Yeah, no leads...it's gone cold and I'm onto the next one."

It sounded as if Darnell was chewing and talking with his mouth full.

"Did I disturb your lunch?"

"Yeah...I mean no. Too busy to go out so I'm eating a leftover bagel from the morning meeting."

"Funny, I'm doing the same thing. Feel like teaming up for a road trip?"

There was a pause on his end, probably him swallowing food.

"Huh...what'd you have in mind?"

"I've been playing around on ViCLAS and found two more M.O.'s that match our shooters...one in Lansing and the other in Port Huron. They have some video footage in PH that might be worth looking at. I can't figure how they might be connected, and remembered how they say two heads are better than one."

Darnell hesitated a couple seconds before responding.

"Okay, you've piqued my interest. Let me run it up the chain here and I'll get back to you. There shouldn't be a problem...my boss has spent half his career in Homicide, and he's a firm believer in interdepartmental cooperation."

"Wish I could say the same for my boss. I look forward to your call...and hey, if anyone from here asks, this was all your idea."

"Don't worry, I got your back."

Abigail hung up and sat back in her chair, polished off the last bite of a granola bar. An alert flashed on the ViCLAS screen. She clicked on the link and was directed to the State of Illinois website. There were three more cases with a similar M.O. in the greater Chicago area. Her eyes widened and her jaw dropped. *Holy shit!*

Nineteen

Partners

They travelled west on I94 in silence. After Darnell picked her up and they exchanged pleasantries, there wasn't much to talk about. It's not like they knew each other well, having only met briefly before. They had the job in common and that was what the Dearborn cop opened with.

"What else have you got besides the ViCLAS link in these homicides?"

She'd been gazing out the window, daydreaming. She turned to Darnell and saw her old partner in his profile. In many ways he was less than Dwayne. Less in height, weight, and looks—definitely looks. What the older brother lacked in appearance he made up for with confidence. She had noticed at the funeral when he read the eulogy and later worked the room.

His personality and demeanor fit the requirements of an older sibling; the son of a war veteran turned Michigan State Trooper. Abigail didn't know much about the father other than the fact he'd been killed on the highway when the boys were young. From what she knew of Darnell, he'd been married and had two children, but was divorced.

"I haven't got much. A hunch mostly, and a possible suspect vehicle that was parked in front of the murder house in downtown Detroit. I had two witnesses, but both managed to get killed."

"What? I heard about the mishap on the freeway. Was that your guy?"

"Yep, reported as an accident while being pursued by police. You remember the two you called Ding and Dong?"

Darnell scanned the road ahead, nodded.

"That was them...the other kid got it in lockup. Our guys had a run-in with the YBN while trying to arrest my suspect. I'm sure the word got back to their homies in jail, that my other guy was a rat. It's not hard to get to someone in there, the gangs practically run the place."

"Christ, Abigail, I can see why you're pissed. I thought things were bad in Dearborn, but you win the shit-show."

She told him about the house, gunshot, and car with a stethoscope and parking permit.

"I'm hoping we can get some corroborating video. My gut tells me the shooter is connected to a hospital or medical facility of some type—maybe a doctor or nurse—someone who wants payback for past aggressions."

"That's not a bad hunch."

The investigator who was in charge of the case in Port Huron was away on vacation. His Lieutenant welcomed Brown and Johnson and set them up in a conference room across the hall from the Detective office. He gave them access to their in-house data base and had the banker's box containing the murder file delivered to them.

Port Huron's digital files made a quick index for finding stuff in the box. Darnell read about the victim and Abigail scanned video clips. The man lived in an upscale condo building with surveillance cameras in and around the block where it was located.

"There!" Brown exclaimed.

A black Chrysler 300. Same kind of car that was at the murder house on Charlevoix."

Johnson leaned over to have a look as she played the clip again.

"Looks like only one in the car...can't tell the gender, and there's no angle on the plate. I don't see any stickers on the windshield, but it looks like beads or something hanging from the rear-view mirror."

"You think it could be a stethoscope?"

Darnell pursed his lips and lifted his brows.

"Don't know...play it again."

He watched closely, turned to Abigail with a flat smile on his face.

"It surely looks like it."

Abigail nodded.

"Anything of use on the vic?"

"Yep, same as mine, registered sex offender. This one was charged with rape, but never convicted. What about your case?"

"Molina was accused of molesting his daughter, but he didn't make the registry. The DA withdrew the charge when the wife and kid never showed up for court...rumour was they skipped town."

The Port Huron Lieutenant was about to pass by their door. He stuck his head in and asked how they were making out. Abigail answered.

"Looks like we might be able to link your suspect vehicle to mine in Detroit, and from what we can tell, the victims are sex offenders. The registry could be a source of info, but we can't say for sure yet. Can we get copies of this stuff?"

"A serial huh? Glad he's moved on. Take copies of whatever you like, and I'll have Wilkinson call you when he's back from Jamaica. It's his case and I'm sure he'll want to coordinate with you. Good work, Detectives."

Twenty

Ducks in a Row

After a quick lunch at a bistro across from the Port Huron police station, Detectives Brown and Johnson went back to their respective offices in Detroit and Dearborn. They both had follow-up paperwork to complete and Abigail wanted to do a chronology of all the cases that they'd linked.

With her wall cleared of Knock-out victims, she pinned up the victims of a serial killer her and Darnell dubbed, *Two-tap.* Major Crimes was quiet, only the Captain was at work in his office. He'd eyed his only female detective through the top of his reading glasses when she came in, but didn't acknowledge her presence.

She studied the geography and timing of the shootings. They'd started in Chicago and moved into Michigan, Detroit being the most recent. There was no visible pattern in the timing of the events.

Abigale and Darnell concurred on the fact that all of the male victims were sex offenders who'd either been suspected of or arrested for a related crime. The fact that interested her the most was that none of the men were convicted of their offences.

Detective Brown sat behind her desk. She stared at the collection of murdered perverts and considered bringing her Captain up to speed. *Fuck him,* she thought, *he'll probably turn her work over to his bum-boys so they can redeem themselves for the shit they caused.* The carbs she'd consumed for lunch weighed on her eyelids. Abigail needed coffee.

The sun beckoned from the window. Deciding a walk would energize her, she threw on her coat, and headed to the café across the street. While the Detective waited for a freshly brewed pot, she gawked at a string of commercials. They appeared in the middle of a cooking show the clerk watched on the TV behind the counter.

Abigail never watched television. She thought it was a waste of time. If she ever turned on the one at home, it was to watch a mindless entertainment, usually a movie, when she didn't want to think about anything in particular. Her eyes shifted from the tube to the coffee pot, and back to the screen. Something caught her attention.

Fuck Me! She stared at the TV as if it was the first time she'd ever seen the invention. The commercial was for Meridian Pharmaceutical, and right there as large as life, was the image that Dion Davies drew for her. It was their company logo.

"Everything okay?" Asked the clerk. "Your coffee's coming right up."

Abigail was on her toes, like a sprinter on the starter block.

"Huh...yeah. I just saw something that made my day. Can I get one of those date squares too, please?"

The clerk handed her the coffee and dessert, knowing her revelation would remain a mystery. Lots of cops came into the café, but few shared anything about the job they did across the street.

Even without the caffeine boost, Abigail covered the distance to her office in half the time. She struggled to get her coat off while she attacked the keyboard on her laptop. The coffee and date square sat untouched on the far corner of her desk. She was on a mission.

Brown brought up the Meridian website and felt a rush. The company had offices in Chicago and Detroit. She immediately thought of calling Darnell, but decided she had to dig further. It was a treasure hunt and the Internet was a great investigative tool. Her fingers trembled while she put pen to paper and scribbled notes. The company's headquarters were downtown, on the Campus Martius square, her next stop.

Detective Brown knew the building, a huge steel and glass skyscraper that towered over the plaza. She craned her neck to see the Meridian name and logo mounted high on the front wall. Abigail shook her head, disappointed she didn't recognize the wiggly letter M. It was the logo that preceded the company name.

Along with a few other tenants, the building housed offices for the pharmaceutical conglomerate. They were Michigan's largest Medicare health plan provider and employed thousands of people. Finding the suspect vehicle and killer, if it was one of their employees, would be like searching for an ingrown toenail on a centipede.

Brown considered calling the company, but with privacy laws and corporate security the way it was, she decided to start at the bottom. There were a few private parking lots and structures on the backside of the building, but she went with her instincts.

A security guard manned the gate to the underground parking lot. Any good cop knows that most people employed by private protection companies are wannabe cops. The rent-a-cop in the booth wore a crisp uniform and looked eager to jump on the first employee who didn't park perfectly between the yellow lines.

In Abigail's experience, she knew that most guards liked to help the cops, hoping they might get a future recommendation for a real job. The young man with private security patches on his shoulders studied the attractive black woman who approached him. She offered her best smile in case he was a hard ass who took his job too seriously.

He melted like butter over hot corn. Within minutes the Detective knew how many vehicles the garage held, its hours of operation, and that it was predominantly executive parking. Other company executives were given privileges on a contractual basis. The security guard said he'd seen lots of black Chrysler

300's going in and out of the garage. They were part of a company fleet used by Meridian sales people who travelled around the state.

Brown patted the young man's arm and held her smile, showing him she was genuinely gratified by the information he'd supplied her. When she pressed him for information on employees who might be driving a particular car, the guard became nervous and said he'd have to refer her to corporate security. That meant a subpoena or search warrant and Abigail knew she lacked the grounds for either.

She asked if she could take a quick spin through the garage, but the kid balked, and apologized. Then came the part that she hated; his sales pitch on why he'd be a great cop, and how much it would mean if someone like her vouched for him.

It was her cue to leave. She called him by name, from the tag on his jacket, and told him she'd keep an eye out for his application when he applied. Against her better judgement, she left him her card.

Abigail drove away with a gut feeling. There was a good chance the serial killer worked for Meridian, and that he or she had access to a Chrysler 300 company vehicle. It was a stretch to prove, but if felt right. A glance at her watch revealed it was quitting time. She wouldn't be able to justify overtime without coming clean with the Captain, and she wasn't ready to let him in on it yet.

When she got back to the office the B & C Team was sitting in the Lieutenant's office. She'd only seen them a few times in the last month. Although Barnes and Campbell were the senior Detectives in the office, they earned their handle after Walker and Tintenelli arrogantly dubbed themselves the A Team. The veteran Detectives were tied up in court all month on a high-profile murder trial.

Abigail was off the clock, but not ready to put her investigation to rest for the day. A thought had come to her when she left Meridian. If she couldn't find out who drove the Chrysler 300 with a stethoscope hanging from the mirror, perhaps she could find out which employees worked in sales. Her hypothesis made sense. If the killer was in sales, they'd be travelling to different places throughout the state.

She scrolled through her contacts and called a woman she knew at Internal Revenue. Her and Gloria exchanged information from time to time, they gotten acquainted when Abigail helped the woman with a stalker. The call went directly to voicemail, her friend was gone for the day.

Detective Brown left a message asking her source to check the income tax files of employees at Meridian, specifically for those claiming travel expenses in Michigan and Illinois. She thanked her friend for the help and said they should get together to catch up. Abigail checked her notes, glanced up at her wall of shame. The Lieutenant locked his office and followed the B & C Team out the door.

Abigail stared at the faces of the murdered victims, one by one. She wondered how they were connected and how the killer knew of them or their crimes. How would a travelling salesman come into such information? Those were questions she wouldn't be able to answer yet. Her calendar reminded her of a dental appointment in the morning. She banged off a quick email to her LT.

The sun had gone home for the night, the dark window was Abigail's cue to do the same.

Twenty-One

Busted

Abigail was still high when she got home; stoked about the progress of her investigation. Where she'd once considered changing the décor in her apartment, it now felt right. The way it did when she put it all together. Her friends told her she had a good eye for design, and some requested her help for their own homes.

The stereo played a smooth jazz station, it was left on while she was at work to make it appear someone was home. The Detective knew it wasn't a true deterrent, but she did it anyway. She also hated the quiet and preferred background noise, usually in the form of music, as proof of life.

Abigail selected a CD and pressed the random button. Enya queued up. She eyed her collection of white wine in the fridge and selected a bottle of Sauvignon Blanc. After pouring a glass, she picked up her phone and called Darnell. She had to tell him about her progress. The call went to voice mail.

Movement outside her balcony door caught her eye. It was snowing. She gazed into evening sky that resembled a charcoal sketch flecked with white dots. In another country beyond the tall buildings that blocked her view south, was a man who'd been in the back of her mind a lot since they last spoke.

She did say she'd call him. Anxious to tell someone her good news, that she was hot on the trail of a serial killer, Norm Strom was her next call. Abigail was about to hang up after the fourth ring, when he answered.

"Hey, did I catch you at a bad time?"

"I was putting the garbage out, my chore for the week."

"It must be nice to be retired and do whatever you want."

"Yep, the best job I've ever had. I have to force myself to get up by the crack of nine, I could sleep until noon. How's the murder case going...the kid give you any more to go on?"

"You won't believe what the fuck happened."

Abigail told Norm about the untimely death of both her suspects and how Walker and Tintenelli screwed things up. She explained she teamed up with her old partner's brother and she had a good lead on the suspect car and her killer might work at Meridian.

"Wow, you've been busy. From what you're saying, it sounds like you're on the right track. But I'm no expert on serial killers."

"Uncle Bill told me something different...said you helped the Mounties hunt one down when you rode up to Alaska. And something else about saving a damsel in distress, that sounds more like you."

Norm chuckled.

"Yeah, that was quite a trip. Got lucky, I guess."

"I'll say."

The conversation fell silent, neither of them knew what to say next. "Well, I just thought I'd call you and fill you in since you were my partner for a few hours. We should get together soon."

"Definitely. Good luck with your case. Let me know how you make out."

"I will. Take care."

Her dental hygienist was good enough to schedule her for the first appointment of the day. It meant she was only an hour late for work, something she could make up over lunch hour. The Lieutenant kept a book to keep track of such things, it saved the department overtime dollars.

Like the flagman at a NASCAR race, her LT waved her into his office the moment Abigail walked in the door.

"You've got some explaining to do, Detective."

His eyed dropped to homicide files that she'd left on her desk. Abigail glanced over her shoulder to her office door, which she'd locked when she left.

"I used my key to enter your office and retrieve these files. I got curious after some kid called...said he was a security guard over at Meridian and he had some information for you on a car you were looking for. He didn't know why, but I solved that mystery when I read these files."

Abigail did a quick head check for the Captain and the A Team. She closed the Lieutenants door behind her and sat down.

"I can explain."

Twenty-Two

Support From Above

Detective Brown poured her heart and soul out to the Lieutenant. She made a point to keep her language in check while she explained how Walker and Tintenelli hijacked a case that she was perfectly capable of handling.

To prove the point, she laid all her cards on his desk and told him about the leads she'd dug up and followed, and her hypothesis about the identification of a serial killer who she believed would probably strike again.

Robinson listened. He checked the files from time to time when his Detective referred to them. She admitted to bringing a Dearborn Detective into the investigation and apologized for not telling him about it.

Then she buttered up her boss by saying she thought *he* had a better handle on what went on in the office than the Captain. He'd made it abundantly clear he didn't like her, and favoured Walker and Tintenelli.

She noticed the Lieutenant nodding his head while she laid it all on the line, and remembered from past interviews that it was a signal he was in agreement. With that in mind, Abigail requested permission to continue her investigation. She said she was close to identifying the killer.

Her LT laced his fingers together and placed his hands on the homicide files. He glanced in the direction of the Captain's office, then laid his eyes on Abigail's. Robinson held his gaze while he gathered the files together in a stack.

"I appreciate your honesty, Detective, but I'm disappointed you went behind my back. Having said that, I accept the fact you were just doing your job, and that you didn't do anything wrong.

In all honesty, I think the Captain's been a bit preoccupied lately, worrying about his next promotion. I would have handled the Walker and Tintenelli caper differently, but it wasn't my call.

I'm going to give you some rope and let you continue your investigation, but make sure you keep me informed every step of the way. I'll update the Captain when I feel it's necessary. Don't worry about those two they've been laying low while. Internal Affairs looked into the deaths of your suspects."

Abigail was surprised to say the least. She hadn't given the Lieutenant enough credit in the past, thought he had no balls. She appreciated his position in middle management.

"Thanks for listening and letting me see this through. You won't be disappointed. Can I continue to include the Detective from Dearborn in my investigation?"

"Do what is necessary to bring the murdering heathen to justice. The good Lord is on your side."

The message light on her phone was flashing when she stepped into her office. After shedding her coat and scarf, unlocking her desk and turning on her computer, Brown listened to her messages. The first one was Darnell, returning her call. He said to call him back when she got in.

The second was from Gloria at the IRS. She said she'd be in and out of meetings all day, but she supplied a list of Meridian employees who'd claimed travel expenses for hotels and meals while on the road for company business. Her friend said it appeared they were using company cars, since there were claims for fuel, but not mileage.

She spelled out five names—four men and one woman. Gloria said all five had changed addresses two years prior, that they were transferred or had moved from Chicago to Detroit. She hoped the information helped and asked Abigail to call her soon, she needed a night out.

Brown considered the list of names. There was one chance in five that the murderer was a woman. She was no expert in the field, but knew that ninety percent of serial killers were men. Abigail dialed Darnell's number, she had to share the news. The LT could be filled in later.

The Dearborn Detective answered and congratulated her on the new leads, but said he was in a hurry and had to leave. He had orders to pick up a prisoner in Lansing and return him for a court appearance. She asked if he could get a copy of the murder file while he was there. Darnell promised he would get it done.

Five names. None of them sounded like serial killers. She recalled reading somewhere how they all had three names, like John Wilkes Booth or Lee Harvey Oswald, or maybe that was only in the case of assassins. One by one, Abigail entered the suspect names into her computer.

The first guy was clean as a whistle with no criminal convictions or traffic tickets, but according to Gloria, he'd been flagged by the IRS for late tax returns.

The second had old convictions for simple drug possession and drunk driving, but nothing in the past fifteen years.

Number three had shoplifting and domestic assault charges that were both settled out of court. She thought it was worth searching his name in other data banks.

Four had a slew of traffic convictions, but nothing criminal.

Five was a female. She was convicted of not wearing her seat belt, and was the victim of a carjacking in which no charges were laid. Abigail pondered a possible scenario and thought it was worth digging into deeper.

Suspect number three was Dale Ford. She sent his name off to the FBI, ViCLAS, and even CPIC, in Canada. Then she Googled his name. Oddly, Ford showed up on a link to the television show, Shark's Den. Abigail clicked more links and found a video clip where Dale Ford pitched his invention of a medical instrument he'd designed. A stethoscope.

Her heart skipped a beat. The Detective watched and learned that Ford had invented a wireless stethoscope. The Sharks were leery of investing because it was untested and they didn't like the fact it came in two pieces. The first piece inserted in the ear like a hearing aid, and the second, a disc the size of a silver dollar, could be kept in a pocket.

Abigail thought it was ingenious, but the separate components would be too easy to misplace, unlike the existing instrument that could be hung around the neck. She watched Ford's demeanor, caught his lack of confidence, he didn't fit the mold of a serial killer. She almost felt sorry for the inventor, switched screens, and saw the other police checks were back. Ford was negative.

She googled the woman, Samantha Evans. There were quite a few hits on the name, most were social media sites like LinkedIn, Facebook, and Pinterest. Abigail wasn't into Facebook, but she clicked on the link to put a face to the suspect's name. There were several women of the same name in Illinois and Michigan, she looked into a few of them, but couldn't confirm anything.

The Detective tried LinkedIn. It was a site for business connections and networking. She found a Samantha Evans who worked for Meridian. Bingo! The picture showed an attractive thirty-something woman with light green eyes and wavy blonde hair that touched her shoulders. It was only a head shot and didn't reveal her body type.

Abigail scrolled down through the woman's accomplishments and interests, and froze. Samantha Evans sat on board of directors for the Sexual Assault Crisis Center.

Twenty-Three

Woman to Woman

Detective Brown jockeyed between her computer and telephone, digging up as much information as she could find on Samantha Evans. As luck would have it, a Sergeant who she'd worked for during her stint in Sex Crimes, sat on the same board as Ms. Evans.

The woman had come highly recommended from the State of Illinois, where she'd held a similar position. The Sergeant knew nothing of the woman personally, so the Detective called the records department of the Chicago Police in an attempt to obtain the carjacking report. She checked her watch while on hold and was astonished it was four in the afternoon.

When the clerk came back on the line Abigail apologized for keeping her at quitting time. Puzzled, the woman said she had to work until four o'clock. Brown checked her watch again and then remembered they were in different time zones. The occurrence was too old to be stored digitally, but the clerk said she'd dig up the paper file and fax her a copy.

The Detective eyed the empty office, confirmed the time on the wall clock. She realized she'd forgotten to eat. Her tummy growled in agreement, she needed sustenance. The vending machines were not an option; too much junk food. Knowing the report from Chicago would take some time, she checked the clock again. Abigail thought the café across the street was open until five and out she went.

The familiar young woman greeted her at the door.

"Oh, I'm sorry, I thought you were open until five."

"Yes, c'mon in, I was just checking on the weather before I head home. Sometimes I sneak out early when it's dead like this. I still have coffee on, but it's been there a while."

"No. I'm good. I was hoping to grab a bite to eat. Do you have any sandwiches left over?"

"All gone, sorry, it was busy in here earlier. I was just prepping a broccoli quiche for tomorrow; do you want me to warm a piece for you?"

"That would be great. Can you make it two? I haven't eaten all day. I'll grab a diet soda out of the fridge."

"Sure, help yourself, it won't be long for the quiche. Is it Gail? Thought I heard one of your co-workers call you that."

"Close. Abigail. And you are?"

"Shareece. Nice to meet you, Detective."

She sat at one on two bistro tables in the window, sipped her soda, and gazed at nothing in particular. Samantha Evans was on her mind. She couldn't wait to see what happened to the woman in Chicago. Was there a catalyst that set her off on a killing spree? If she really was the killer, were her victims connected in some way? They were all from different walks of life with nothing in common.

Shareece delivered the quiche with a Colgate smile; she could have put a straw through the gap in her front teeth.

"Here you go. You gotta eat, put some meat on them bones."

The girl was almost twice Abigail's size, but her high cheekbones gave her a doll face. The detective put the business end of her fork to work.

"Couldn't wait til you got home to eat?"

Abigail tried not to spew chunks when she answered with her mouth full.

"I'm still working."

"Didn't think they had the money to pay you overtime."

"They don't. It's an important case...a murder."

Shareece slapped her hand over her heart, as if she had just been shot.

"Oh my God that's terrible. Don't know how you do it girl. I'd pee my pants seein someone dead like that."

Brown was into the second piece of quiche, she washed it down with soda. Her wheels were spinning. Samantha Evans was in her head. Shareece came out from behind the counter with a broom and swept the area around Abigail's table. Looking down at the crumbs that escaped her mouth she felt embarrassed. The woman had probably finished cleaning up before she came in.

"Don't fret none, looks like you enjoyed the pie."

"Just what I needed, thanks."

Abigail used her hand and swept any leftover crumbs from the table onto her plate. Her phone rang. It was Darnell.

"Hey, I'm done for the day, thought I'd check in before I take off. What do you want me to do with the Lansing file?"

"You got it...great. I don't need it right away, maybe we can get together tomorrow. I got..."

The low battery signal beeped on her phone.

"...a good suspect, but need to tie in the Vics. Let me get back to you later, my phone's dying and I'm gonna lose you."

"No problem. Catch you later."

She asked Shareece how much for the quiche and coke.

"Don't you worry, I can write it off as waste. I like to help the police whenever I can. They don't pay you folks enough for what you do."

"Thank-you, but you didn't have to do that."

She dropped a sawbuck on the table and bundled up.

"Thanks again. You take care."

"You too."

Twenty-Four

Pick of the Litter

Samantha Evans felt a tightness in her chest and took a deep breath. There was nothing physically wrong with her, it happened every time she browsed the list of names. They were all sex offenders, registered in a system that kept track of their whereabouts. An attempt to keep society informed and safe. It was an insult to everyone as far as she was concerned.

She had just received the new list, with current addresses, of the city's worst predators. It was her job as a board member for the Sexual Assault Crisis Center to monitor these sick perverts. Evans had been on the board in Chicago. When the pharmaceutical company transferred her to Detroit, she accepted a similar position.

The job had her on the road a lot. She had time to give as a director, and that served a dual purpose for her. As a concerned citizen, it was her way to help the victims of sex crimes. It was also personal; an avenue to gain retribution for those abused by criminals and the courts. It wasn't only for the vicious assaults on others. It was payback for the heinous crime she endured.

In the beginning she felt like a vigilante, and told herself it was for the benefit of all the other victims. After the first one, she realized it was an act of vengeance and a big part of her healing process. Samantha was killing her way to recovery and felt a little bit better every time she squeezed the trigger, and watched someone else feel pain.

Perusing the list made her feel nauseous, especially when she considered the number of sexual deviates who lived among decent people; the quiet neighbor who never bothers anyone and is accepted as an equal. Picking her victims wasn't difficult.

There were always a few who beat the system and paid nothing for their crimes. They were fair game. Her prey.

Evans didn't consider what she did as murder. To her it was more of a public service. Her victims weren't missed by anyone, and the police who investigated were taxed with more important matters. They didn't seem too concerned when a pervert bit the dust. Secretly, she thought the police admired what she was doing and would like to do it themselves. It was justifiable homicide.

She vomited the first time she shot a man in the crotch and blew his balls to pieces. The second shot to the chest followed quickly with remorse for the suffering she caused another human being. While cleaning up the mess, the feeling of sorrow dissipated and anger took over.

It was the memory of her own downfall that infuriated her. How naïve she was. How easily she became a victim. Too much to drink that night didn't help. She should have taken a cab, but she didn't want to leave the company car unattended in a seedy neighborhood.

Samantha never saw her attacker. He grabbed her from behind and pushed her into the car. The details were vague. She remembered her face bouncing off the steering wheel. When she awoke in the hospital, they told her she'd been raped, and was found lying unconscious in a parking lot. Her attacker stole the car.

Miraculously, police arrested a suspect and they summoned her to court. Evans soon discovered that the accused had more rights than the victim. The defense attorney made her out to be a drunken slut who dressed provocatively and should have known better. Thread by thread, the case unravelled. DNA was the key evidence, but it was proven the chain of continuity had been broken, and it was disallowed.

Since Samantha didn't see her attacker, there was nothing to place him at the scene. The car was found abandoned and torched. She almost fainted when the Judge dismissed the case. The accused shouted and pumped his fist in the air, as if he'd just scored a touchdown. In a way he did.

It took almost a year for Evans to recover enough to travel on her own again. During that time, she met some great people at the Sexual Assault Crisis Center. She volunteered her time to be with other women who were victims of crime. It helped her healing process. Another year later, she took the opening on the Board of Directors.

Samantha was blown away the first time she saw the long list of sexual predators. They were living among people unaware of them or their crimes. Her eyes almost popped out of her head when she saw his name, the man who raped her and changed her life forever. He had to pay.

She got a gun and practiced with it at the shooting range after the assault. It was a larger calibre than the seller recommended, but she loved the feeling of power and exhilaration that came with each pull of the trigger. It had to be a reflex when she got sick after killing her abuser. Maybe it had something to do with the rush of adrenaline. She never saw a dead person before, let alone killed one.

Evans was a nervous wreck for weeks after she did the deed, thinking the police would arrest her after they discovered she was a previous victim. How stupid could she be? It would only be a matter of time. But the cops never came, and she wasn't even questioned.

It was a few months later when she asked a Police Lieutenant who was on the same board why the man had been omitted from their list. She almost peed herself when he said the man had been murdered by a woman he sexually abused. They believed she was a prostitute and the deal went bad. His neighbors said working girls visited him regularly and he would sometimes slap them around. Investigators figured he met his match.

After that, Samantha kept her distance. She went after offenders who couldn't be connected to her. She had to be smart. The list was extensive in Illinois and Michigan, and she had no problem selecting worthy victims. The worst offenders became her targets. The hunted became the hunter.

Twenty-Five

Smooth Jazz

The fax machine had run out of paper while printing the file from Chicago. Abigail stuffed more into the machine and it continued spewing pages. She went through her routine of closing up shop, the Detective planned on taking the file home to read. About to shut down her computer, the email icon caught her eye.

Her friend in Sex Crimes sent her the most recent list of registered offenders. She was one step ahead of Brown and thought the suspect was choosing her victims from that collection of perverts. Abigail sent the email to the printer. At home, with soft music in the background, and a glass of wine in her hand, she would piece it all together.

Chris Botti's trumpet was unmistakable, he was another musician Norm Strom introduced to her. Abigail loved the sound of brass and preferred instrumentals when she was trying to think. Curious, she skimmed the list of sex offenders. Alberto Molina's name was among them.

She remembered reading about his crime when she checked on Walker and Tintenelli's follow up investigation. They'd dug up a reported child abuse. Molina was accused of molesting his stepdaughter. He was arrested and charged, but never convicted. The girl was mentally challenged, and deemed to be an unreliable witness. Regardless of the dismissal, he was on the list.

Keeping that in mind, Abigail read the fax reports she had on Samantha Evans' sexual assault. The case was weak from the start. She was amazed that police came up with a suspect. Brown knew what it was like to lose on a technicality. All too often, there was no justice in the justice system.

She sympathized with the woman and couldn't imagine the pain she felt after being assaulted, and again when she watched her abuser walk away as if it never happened. That was the catalyst. Abigail wondered if Samantha's abuser was her first victim. The Detective noted dates and case numbers. She would have to call Chicago again to see if he was still alive.

The murders in both states took place while the suspect lived in each of them. The Lansing and Port Huron victims were not in Abigail's jurisdiction, and their names were not on the Detroit list. She figured Evans got their names through her connections. It seemed the woman was more vigilante than serial killer.

Who is that playing the alto sax? She wondered, but couldn't remember. The Detective made a note to check for firearm registrations in Evans' name in Illinois and Michigan. If that failed, she would obtain warrants to search her car and home. She thought she'd put together a good circumstantial case, and had enough to question the suspect, but hard evidence would give her grounds to make an arrest.

* * *

Smooth jazz played on FM 98.7 in Samantha Evans' car. To her, the soothing sound was as relaxing as a cigarette after sex. She'd just done the deed, putting down another predator, like a rabid dog. It was exhilarating. Gun powder residue clung to the hairs in her nose. She took a deep breath, and another look around the neighborhood as she drove away.

His name was different than the others, the story the same. Raymond Gonzalez, convicted of gang-rape, testified against his accomplices in three unsolved gang-related murders. He was sentenced to time served and put on probation with the condition he remain in his residence. Samantha scoffed when she saw the monitoring device strapped to his ankle. He was a rapist and a rat; the world would be a better place without him.

It was the same after each of her justified executions. She was not ready to come down from the euphoria. She stopped by a cocktail lounge frequented by executive types. She met men there before, and used them for her own gratification. Evans had no interest in a relationship with any man.

Easy to look at, she never had to pay for a drink. Her casual attire clung in all the right places and heads turned wherever she went. Still flushed from her high, Samantha loosened her scarf, and entered the bar.

After checking herself from head to toe, she aimed for the gaggle of suits at the bar. Wearing a smile that was a half smirk, she pondered who the lucky one would be. Who would fuck the man-killer?

Twenty-Six

Bad Karma

Abigail planned the day in her head while on her morning run. She felt confident it was her time to catch a killer. She felt like everyone's eyes were on her when she strolled into the station, and took the elevator up to the third floor.

Major Crimes was busier than usual, The B & C team were in with the Captain. Brown recognized an officer from Forensics, in with the Lieutenant.

She exchanged nods with the LT and entered her office. While shedding her coat Abigail saw the message light on her phone. The Detective put her coffee and the files she brought from home on the desk, and powered up her computer. Her thoughts were all about taking down Samantha Evans. She checked the phone messages.

Darnell Johnson called just after she left the day before. He apologized for not being more available, and said he was tied up investigating a string of home invasions. There was a message from her Uncle Bill. He was an early riser who got up at the crack of dawn. He said he wanted to catch up and was available for lunch if she had the time.

With the phone still in her hand, Detective Brown called someone she knew at the ATF. The call went to voicemail so she left a message with her contact asking them to check for permits in the name of Samantha Evans. Before taking her investigation any further, Abigail thought it was time to bring her LT up to speed. The Forensic Technician had just left his office.

She took a sip of coffee and walked with her cup over to the Lieutenants office.

"Good morning, Abigail, I was hoping you had an update for me. There are more cases coming in every day. Just last night..."

Excited, and confident she was about to bring down a serial killer, she cut him off.

"Yes, sir, that's what I'm here to tell you...I have a good case and have narrowed it down to one suspect. A woman, if you can believe it?"

"Really?"

"Yes. Everything fits...dates, locations, and her connection to the victims. And she was a victim of sexual assault. I believe it's the reason she's killing certain men. Rapists and deviates who are on the offenders list, she has access to it. I'm checking for gun permits in her name right now, Samantha Evans. I want to do a search warrant..."

Lieutenant Robinson held up a hand and leaned forward in his chair.

"Did you say Samantha Evans?"

Something clicked in the back of her head. Abigail scanned the office, but didn't see Walker or Tintenelli. Her eyes bulged, she wanted to lunge at her boss.

"What did those assholes do now? I thought you were letting me run with this investigation? This is fucking bullshit, LT, why don't you just transfer me out of this shithole? I've had enough!"

Robinson fell back into his chair and put both hands up, signalling the Detective to slow down.

"Easy, Abigail, they're only following orders. I called them in early this morning."

Abigail was so worked up she'd squeezed her coffee cup to the point that the liquid spilled over her hand. It was hot and burned, but she ignored the pain.

"Were they snooping in my case files again? Can't come up with *their* own leads?"

He pushed the air with both hands, signalling her to calm down.

"Detective Brown, if you'd calm down a minute and refrain from the use of vulgar language, I can explain to you what your fellow Detectives are doing. Not that I'm obliged to. It appears we have some sort of misunderstanding. I asked you about Samantha Jones because she's dead. That's what their working on."

"What? I don't understand...she's my number one suspect. That doesn't make any sense. She's the killer, not a victim. What the hell happened?"

"It's too early to know for sure, the body was found in her car. It was parked near a cocktail lounge where business executives hang out. Walker says it looks like a sexual encounter that went bad—she was strangled to death."

"You gotta be shitting me. Did they find a gun?"

The Lieutenant raised his eyebrows, as if the question surprised him.

"Yes, a big one under the front seat. The ballistics expert just left here, says it's the same calibre used in the Molina homicide, but he hasn't done a comparison yet. Once the results are back you can have them do comparisons in the other cases you connected."

Abigail was in shock. She shook her head, couldn't speak.

"Tintenelli says she frequents the bar and has left there with men before. It sounds like a pickup place. Your suspect was there for that purpose. If she was a serial killer, it seems that the good Lord has intervened and put an end to her wickedness. He does work in mysterious ways."

Silent, Brown stood up and dropped her coffee cup into the trash can beside Robinson's desk. As if she was a preprogrammed robot, the Detective turned and walked back to her office. Abigail felt like a punching bag that just had the stuffing knocked out of it. She slumped into her chair and stared into the empty space in front of her.

Twenty-Seven

Loose Ends

The five miles seemed like fifteen. Abigail replayed the scene in the Lieutenant's office in her head. She tried to recall what she did the rest of that day, but couldn't remember. She finished the day and left for home in a fog. One thing remained clear in her mind, Samantha Evans was dead, and so was her case. The only thing left for her to do was write off the other homicides to her.

She sprinted the last eighth of a mile to clear her head and leave the case behind like her tracks on the sidewalk. Spring would arrive as surely as new cases to work on. And there was still that stack of old burglary files the Captain would be asking her about. It was life in the big city. One killer whacked by another killer. Not the first time that happened.

Abigail expected to be greeted with stupid looks and comments when she entered the Major Crimes office. It didn't happen. She wasn't early as usual. What was the point? Walker and Tintenelli had their heads buried in paperwork. The Captain was MIA, no surprise there. Lieutenant Robinson was on the phone in his office, he waved her over.

He hung up when she stepped into his office.

"Good morning. Please sit down. I just got off the phone with my counterpart in Port Huron. Someone from Lansing called too, and I would imagine the Chicago Police will be grateful as well. You did a good job, Detective. I know you're disappointed with how things turned out, but you did more than close files. Those victims had families."

"Do you really think those perverts were missed by their families, LT?"

"The good Lord loves all his children. If they asked for forgiveness, it was granted."

Brown pulled off her scarf and unbuttoned her coat. She retrieved her coffee from the edge of Robinson's desk, and cupped it with both hands.

"I know you believe that. I'm sorry, but I can't."

He nodded, glanced over to the self-proclaimed A Team.

"They might not show it, but Walker and Tintenelli appreciate your work on the Molina case. They could use your help to tie up loose ends. You spent a lot of time working up a background on Samantha Evans. I'd like you to give them whatever you have on her so they can close the file."

Abigail remained silent, suppressed the urge to object, and be a whiner. She was better than that. Like a good soldier, the Detective nodded in agreement, and left the Lieutenant's office. She walked to hers and hung up her coat. After gathering any paper she had on Samantha Evans, Brown photocopied her notes.

It felt as if she was turning in homework to her teacher. Walker didn't look up, he ignored her as usual. She handed everything she had to Tintenelli. His gaze softer than usual, his nod a silent thank-you. An evidence bag that contained Evans' personal belongings sat on top of the murder scene photos. Abigail's eyes locked on Tintenelli's.

"Do you mind if I have a look at the evidence?"

Tintenelli slid the pile closer to her.

"Go ahead, help yourself."

The pictures were self-explanatory. She saw the black Chrysler 300 she'd been trying to locate, with Samantha Evans lying face up, across the front seats. Her clothes were disheveled, but still intact—odd for a rape. There were ligature marks on her neck, just above a thin necklace. She hated to ask the A Team anything, but was curious.

"I thought she was raped, what's with her clothes?"

Walker continued to ignore her.

Tintenelli answered. "Semen in her mouth and on her left hand. Looks like a blow-job that got out of hand, so to speak."

She thought about that, flipped through the remaining photographs. Abigail picked up the bag of jewelry. It was all high-end stuff, with the exception of the necklace. A small black stone pendant hung on a single strand of twisted leather, like native artwork. Abigail returned everything to its place and turned to leave.

"Oh, I didn't see it in the photos. Was there a stethoscope hanging from her mirror?"

Walker and Tintenelli both raised their heads and eyeballed each other.

Tintenelli responded. "No, why? Was she a doctor or something?"

Abigail paused for a second.

"It's not important. Nothing to worry about."

Brown headed back to her office when Walker's voice clucked her in the back of the head. Abigail shortened her stride, trying to decide whether to turn around. She did.

"Nice work, Detective."

She offered a flat smile, nodded. When she got back to her desk, she called the medical examiner. Something in the crime scene photos gnawed at her. The doctor said he could see her after lunch.

Abigail met Uncle Bill for lunch at the diner across the street. She had to talk him out of Lafayette Coney Island, his favorite eatery. She had a bowl of broccoli-cheddar soup and a tuna salad wrap. He ate a clubhouse and kettle chips. She exchanged pleasantries with Shareece when she got there, but the waitress was busy with other lunch orders.

Abigail and Uncle Bill caught up between bites, he wanted to know all the details of how his niece took down the vigilante serial killer. He knew she didn't feel appreciated in Major Crimes, and tried to cheer her up by telling her of his conversation with his old partner, the Chief. There were changes coming down the pipe. She should bide her time and continue doing her job. Her turn would come.

Uncle Bill asked Abigail if she'd seen or heard from Norm Strom. He added his two cents about how he thought they made a good pair, and how she could use a good man in her life to keep her grounded. The conversation about how she needed a man came up from time to time. She knew he meant well.

Brown thought about the dead body on the stainless-steel table. She saw plenty of them, and never had a problem keeping her lunch down. The morgue smell was unique and something you never forgot once experienced. The Medical Examiner gave Abigail an overview of his autopsy. She took a close look at the ligature marks on the neck, but something was amiss.

"Good eye, Detective. Those marks aren't normal for strangulation. Most occur from behind with the thumbs on the back of the neck. This woman was strangled from the front, probably while staring at her killer. His grip was powerful and his thumbs broke the hyoid bone."

Brown focussed on the neck just above the collar bone. The doctor pointed to the area closer to the chin.

"The hyoid is further up."

"I'm aware. In the crime scene photos she's wearing a leather necklace, but I don't see any marks on her skin from it assuming that would be the case in a violent strangulation."

The ME took a closer look at the neck.

"You could be right, but it was the thumbs and pressure to the hyoid that caused hypoxia and death. The necklace wouldn't have made a difference to the injury."

"Thank-you, Doctor. Can you confirm there was no vaginal penetration or rape?"

"Yes, no signs of trauma. In my opinion, she was orally copulating her assailant when he strangled her. Semen in her mouth would indicate he ejaculated at some point during the attack."

Abigail scanned the remainder of the body, jotted down a few notes, and thanked the ME for his time.

On the drive back to the station, she thought about the conversation with her uncle about Norm Strom. Erotic visions came to mind. It had been a long time since she'd had been with him, or any man for that matter.

The sun reflected off the glass buildings in the downtown core. Abigail rolled down her window and filled her lungs with fresh air. She smelled the river, and maybe just a hint of spring.

Twenty-Eight

The Beat Goes On

Alberto Molina and Samantha Evans were only names in her notebook and bytes of data in police files. The dust settled and any accolades for a job well done were now memories.

Abigail was assigned new cases, and continued to work on her old files with a dull chisel. The work was monotonous. She needed a vacation. With no plan or destination in mind, she applied for, and was given a week off.

Her first call was to Norm Strom. She asked about getting together, but he said he was busy doing laundry and watching the paint dry on a piece of wood he crafted. When she said she had a week off, he surprised her by suggesting a getaway.

"Really. What makes you think I want to go away with you?"

"You called me, probably out of desperation, me being the last name on your list and all."

Abigail laughed.

"What can I say, I miss my partner in crime."

Norm laid out a plan. He suggested she come over for dinner, bring her jammies, and if they still liked each other in the morning, head to Stratford for a few days. He mentioned all the little cool towns in the area, and described how Stratford released swans into the Avon River every spring.

She'd already packed a bag, hoping he say yes and invite her over for dinner. The man could cook, and not only in the kitchen. The drive was a blur, except for a quick stop to pick up some wine. It was the least she could do. Norm greeted her at his front door, and exchanged her bag for a glass of Sauvignon Blanc. He paired the wine with the first course.

The booze and conversation flowed easily. They talked about Stratford and other places they both wanted to see. As an appetizer, he served bacon wrapped scallops, with a touch of maple syrup and cinnamon. Abigail scanned the open-style kitchen and living area, while Nora Jones played on the stereo.

"You have good taste in décor, for a man. You sure you're not gay?"

Norm smirked.

"If that's the case you won't be getting dessert."

She had a good idea where his thoughts and the conversation were going. She played along.

"Something white, and sweet, perhaps?"

"It's a surprise, you've had it before."

Norm left her hanging, added fresh bacon bits and dressing to the Caesar salad. He was removing two bowls from the cupboard when her phone rang. Abigail checked the call display.

"Shit! Its work...don't they know I'm on vacation?"

She answered the call, acknowledged Lieutenant Robinson, and said a lot of yes sirs and okay's, and thankyous. Norm watched the expression on Abigail's face go from happy to confused, to one of concern. He worked the cork on a bottle of Rose that paired with the salad.

Abigail ended the call. Her eyes drooped and the corners of her mouth curled as if a family member died. Then she sniffed the air and put on her cop face. Norm had seen it many times over the years—the look of someone who meant business. She reached for her glass of wine and pushed it away.

"What's going on? Are we still having dinner?"

Brown hesitated for a moment, stepped closer and wrapped her arms around Norm's neck. She brought her mouth to his and kissed him passionately. He responded in kind, remembering how soft her lips were and how good it felt to hold her. Abigail moaned, then pulled back and looked him in the eyes.

"I'm so sorry. I have to go to work."

"What? I thought we were..."

"My Lieutenant called me in for a homicide. They think it's linked to the woman serial killer. The one that was killed. He apologized for calling me on vacation, but said his orders came from above. The new Commander likes the way I handled things and wants me to take the lead on this one. They bumped me up a grade in rank, but there'll be no extra cash until the new budget comes in."

Abigail gathered her things while she explained. Norm pouted like a dog who just had his favorite bone taken away.

"This really sucks. It used to be me that had to bail, back in the days when I worked for a living."

"I know baby. Maybe I can get back, but shit, who knows when? You know what it's like the first forty-eight. I'm really sorry, I was really wanted and needed this...and more."

Abigail grabbed him and kissed him again. Norm melted.

"You're killing me. You better come back. Call me when you can."

She shifted her eyes from his to the food and back to him.

"It's killing me too. I was looking forward to dinner...and *dessert*. Rain check?"

"While supplies last, don't wait too long, there's an expiration date. Just kidding, get back here when you can."

Norm opened the front door. There would be no hot chocolate for dessert. She brushed past him and turned to blow a kiss.

"Take care, my white knight."

Author Bio

Ed grew up in Windsor Ontario, in Canada. He joined the Windsor Police Department in 1977, a month before his nineteenth birthday. After almost two years as a police cadet, Ed was promoted to Constable and he walked a beat in downtown Windsor. He spent the next thirteen years in uniform working the front lines.

From there, he was transferred to plain clothes where he worked in narcotics, morality, property crimes, fraud, and arson. During his time as a Detective, Ed investigated everything from theft and burglary to arson and murder. He retired as a Detective with a total of thirty-one years and four months service.

Within weeks of retirement Ed took to travelling the world, visiting countries in Southeast Asia and South America as well as riding his motorcycle all over Canada and the United States. He kept in touch with family and friends through email, sending them snippets and stories of his adventures.

The recipients of his musings suggested he write a book about his travels and Ed complied by putting together a collection of short stories in his first book, A Casual Traveler. The book was well received. Having been bitten by the writing bug, Ed decided to share some of his police stories.

He created the Norm Strom crime fiction series, based on events and people he'd encountered during his years in law enforcement. Ed wrote and self-published Rat, Bloody Friday, Torch, and Finding Hope. He joined fellow authors Christian

Edmond Gagnon

Laforet and Ben Van Dongen in putting together a crime anthology, All These Crooked Streets.

Ed continues to write, adding this book to his Norm Strom novels. He also wrote a science fiction thriller called, Four. Ed still travels frequently and resides in Windsor with his wife, Cathryn.

You can see all of Ed's books and his travel blog at:
www.edmondgagnon.com